A DANGEROUS LOVE

To make way for a new industrial park, Janie Tempest is being forced to move from her cottage. It had been left to her by her godmother, Aunt Jane, and this is resented by Brian Cook, her aunt's step-nephew, who had once tried to make love to Janie. When the removal company let Janie down at the last minute, the men who are moving her neighbour's things offer to help. One of them, the handsome and disturbing Manuel, asks Janie out to dinner. Then Brian turns up with what he claims is a new will leaving everything to him . . .

Books by Livvy West
in the Linford Romance Library:

HER CAPTIVE CAVALIER
THE BLAZING GLEN

LIVVY WEST

A DANGEROUS LOVE

Complete and Unabridged

LINFORD
Leicester

First published in Great Britain in 2004

First Linford Edition
published 2005

British Library CIP Data

West, Livvy
   A dangerous love.—Large print ed.—
Linford romance library
   1. Love stories
   2. Large type books
   I. Title
   823.9'14 [F]

   ISBN 1–84395–821–X

Published by
F. A. Thorpe (Publishing)
Anstey, Leicestershire

Set by Words & Graphics Ltd.
Anstey, Leicestershire
Printed and bound in Great Britain by
T. J. International Ltd., Padstow, Cornwall

This book is printed on acid-free paper

1

Janie looked at the phone receiver in disbelief as she tried to take in what the caller was saying.

'What do you mean, you can't come? You'll be late?' she added hopefully.

'No, love, we can't come at all today. Overbooked, see, and the other small van's broken down coming back from a job yesterday. Friday's the first we can manage.'

She took a deep breath. This couldn't be happening. It was a drama, a nightmare.

'But I have to be out of here by tomorrow at the latest. Tomorrow, Wednesday. You know that! I told him, your boss, when I booked you. And he promised! Put me through to the manager.'

'Sorry, love, he's driving one of the vans. Jack's off sick, see.'

For ten minutes she argued, pleaded, threatened, and almost cried, but it did no good. Friday was the earliest they could come, and the bulldozers would be here on Thursday.

Janie raked her fingers through her hair and grabbed the Yellow Pages. Thank goodness she hadn't packed that. Had it been a premonition? Tugging the belt of her bathrobe tighter, she abandoned the idea of a shower. She had more urgent things to do.

For sixty frustrating minutes during which she became even more desperate, she rang every removal company within a radius of thirty miles. None could help.

What on earth could she do? Who could help her move her big pieces of furniture? Most of her friends lived some distance away, and none of them had big enough cars anyway, or they would be at work. That reminded her of Liz. Her sister temped, and as often as not had no job to go to. Hadn't she mentioned a new boyfriend with a big estate car? Even though Liz lived twenty miles away, north of Bristol, that would be better than nothing. It was a forlorn hope, but it was one.

She dialled, but there was no reply. Liz might be at work. She'd try her later in case she'd just been out shopping, but meanwhile she was cast back on her own resources. They were limited. If she hired a roof-rack, could she get any of her furniture on it?

She went to the window to look at her tiny car sitting outside the cottage, though she already knew it would not hold the larger pieces of furniture that were left. A roof-rack would mean half a dozen separate trips, and in any case she doubted if she could get the wardrobe or the bed downstairs on her own, and she certainly couldn't lift them on to a rack. She might, however, persuade a friend to help later that evening, when they were home from work. She'd leave messages with those who had answerphones, or get them on mobiles.

For a crazy, desperate moment she wondered whether to appeal to Brian. He worked for a big transport firm near Avonmouth docks, and no doubt had access to all sorts of vehicles. Then she dismissed the idea. He'd be busy, and even if he wasn't he'd delight in refusing to help her. The days when he'd tried to become more than a casual acquaintance were long past, and he'd taken her rejection of his overtures badly. They met occasionally, living in the same area, but had no closer relationship.

Once more she considered the possibilities of her car. With the back seats down it was quite roomy. She'd already moved the boxes, the books and china and chairs. Even the armchair had gone into it. True, she'd had to leave the tail-gate open when she took her kitchen table, and there was no way she could get her bed, the settee, or the wardrobe in even if she could haul them that far.

She was reaching for her address book when a loud, imperious voice caught her attention.

'Do be careful, man!'

'It's OK, keep your hair on.'

Janie glanced through the window and saw her neighbour, the rather superior Mrs Kemp, standing on the circular gravel drive in front of her house. She was gesticulating as two large men carried out something shrouded in a grey blanket. Most of Mrs Kemp's stuff had gone yesterday in two huge pantechnicons, but she'd mentioned the last of it would be taken today. They had a small van parked in the drive, so close to the house Janie hadn't noticed it before. She felt a surge of hope. Perhaps, when they had moved Mrs Kemp's things they would be able to do hers. She had very little left, only a few big items. They wouldn't take long.

She almost tripped over the doorstep in her haste, and saved herself by clutching at the door knob. The door swung to, the latch clicking, but Janie scarcely registered it as she ran down the path and along the grass verge towards her neighbour's house.

As she reached the van one of the furniture removers stepped back and collided with her.

'Oof!'

Janie, winded, came to an involuntary halt. She'd have fallen if he hadn't grabbed her round the waist.

'You OK?'

He had a deep voice, with a slightly foreign intonation. It wasn't quite American, but she couldn't identify it.

Janie glanced up at him, struggling to regain her breath. His hair was black, his skin deeply tanned, and he had the bluest eyes she'd ever seen. She was tall, but she only came up to his shoulder. She wondered if he had Mediterranean blood. He was dark enough. Was his accent Italian, or Spanish, perhaps?

Before she could decide, Mrs Kemp's acid tones brought her back to the present.

'Janie, my dear child, is the house on fire?' Mrs Kemp demanded. 'And aren't you dressed yet? You are always so impetuous. Tempest by name, and tempest by nature.'

'Sorry,' Janie gasped.

She felt guilty of all sorts of unmentionable sins, and blushed furiously. And what was she doing, admiring the good looks of a furniture removal man and trying to identify an accent when she had far more important things to think about? Mrs Kemp sniffed.

'You never think before you act.'

She was the widow of a colonel, prim and proper. If there were any good works to be done Mrs Kemp would be at the front of the queue, Janie often thought, especially if these voluntary jobs entailed telling everyone else what to do. She treated everyone, but especially Janie, as though they were raw, incompetent squaddies. However much Janie tried, the woman always had this demoralising effect on her, and being half naked as well as crashing into the handsome furniture man didn't help, nor did the grin on the broad, red face of the other man, who was wiping sweat off his brow.

'My removal firm has let me down. They say they can't come till Friday, and I can't find anyone else. I wondered, that is, I hoped, that these men could fit in a small, extra job. I haven't got much,' she added, turning to the men with a nervous smile.

She realised, seeing his face in close-up, that the good-looking one still had his arm round her waist, and wriggled in embarrassment. He grinned at her and let her go, and she suppressed the desire to slap the smile from his handsome face. No doubt he considered his film-star looks gave him all sorts of advantages with women. He was being too familiar, and she didn't permit familiarities from strangers. On the other hand she was desperate, and she needed him.

'But that's not possible,' Mrs Kemp

began, and Janie swung round to face her.

'Please, I don't know what else to do. If I'm not out of here by tomorrow they'll bulldoze the furniture as well. I'll pay overtime, double rates, anything!' she added, looking at the men.

'Janie, you don't understand,' Mrs Kemp said, but the dark-haired one spoke over her.

'Sure, we can do it. OK with you, Tim?'

The other man nodded, and Janie sighed deeply.

'I'm so grateful.'

'But Janie — ' Mrs Kemp began again.

Once more he interrupted.

'This afternoon, we'll come back after we've settled Mrs Kemp's job.'

Janie practically gibbered with relief.

'Thank you so much! I just didn't know what to do. I'll take all my small last-minute stuff round now. It's only a couple of miles away. See you later.'

She walked towards her own front

door, not heeding the muttering from Mrs Kemp. She could do without a lecture about decorum, proper modes of dress, and being too forward. If she permitted Mrs Kemp to start, all these topics would be mentioned. The woman had brought all of them, and more, into the conversation the day after Janie's housewarming party. On the whole she was kind-hearted, but Janie had only been there for a couple of years, and they were too different in age and outlook to have made friends.

She'd need more cash as they'd want paying in cash. A visit to the bank was on the cards, then, and she'd do some shopping, stock up at the supermarket. Luckily she'd already taken her fridge to the new house. She could put away her shopping, take the clothes and bedding she'd needed until today, maybe start to sort out her new kitchen.

She sighed. She'd loved this cottage, ever since she'd spent holidays with Aunt Jane as a child. It was like a fairytale cottage in her books. There were windows either side of the front door, and small ones above peeping out from under the thatch. Inside it was all dark beams and stone walls, the rooms leading into each other, full of antiques.

Outside, roses climbed round the door, and the garden was full of old-fashioned plants, mostly perfumed, such as lavender, verbena, honeysuckle and mock orange. They gave off delicious scents in summer, and the garden had been Aunt Jane's delight. Janie suspected it had taken the place of her only son, who had died years ago in a boating accident.

She wasn't a real aunt, but she was Janie's godmother, and it had been a total surprise when she had left Janie the cottage, one she had never expected but which had thrilled her. Even Brian's fury at being cut out of the will had not spoiled her joy at this wonderful gift. He'd had no claim on Aunt Jane in any case. It had taken the planners to ruin the idyllic life she'd planned.

Janie suddenly realised she had been

standing on the step, daydreaming, for ages, twisting the unresponsive knob. The door wouldn't open! She swore inwardly. In her haste she hadn't slipped the catch, and the lock had clicked to behind her. Were any of the windows open? It was a cold day, typical February weather, and her bedroom window was open, but none of the ground floor windows. She shivered suddenly. She'd rushed out without thinking, and her bathrobe wasn't keeping out the biting wind.

She'd have to break in. At least she wouldn't need to repair the window. But she'd do it round at the back, where no-one could see what she was doing. And, she admitted with a wry smile, where Mrs Kemp and her removal men would not witness another example of her idiocy.

Glancing round to make sure they weren't observing her discomfort, she chose a moment when they all disappeared into the house and slid hastily round to the back of her cottage. The kitchen window, a casement, was the biggest, and if she broke the pane nearest the catch she could reach in to open it. Then, with the help of a few bricks, those left over from some repairs years ago, she could clamber in.

A small platform was soon constructed, and Janie took the topmost brick, smashed the glass, and leaned in to grasp the handle. It was stiff, and at an awkward angle, but she eventually yanked it down and pulled the window open.

She hitched up the skirts of her robe, wishing again she'd stopped to pull on some proper clothes, and had her knee on the sill when she heard footsteps pounding on the gravel path. Strong hands seized her round the waist and dragged her backwards. For a few moments she lay against a warm, well-muscled body, then she struggled to release herself.

'What do you think you're doing?' she demanded, twisting round and looking up into blue eyes, which were crinkling in amusement.

'That's my question. Are you mad? You could injure yourself badly if you fell down inside, or cut yourself on the glass. And you might be lying there for hours until I came back.'

She gritted her teeth and swallowed her hasty retort. She couldn't afford to antagonise him, as he was going to do her an enormous favour.

'The front door slammed shut, and I didn't have my key. And I'm quite capable of climbing through a window.'

'Not in skirts which will trip you up any minute. I'll do it.'

To her fury, he picked her up as though she weighed no more than a child, swung her round, and deposited her a yard away. Before she could regain her breath he had one leg over the windowsill and was easing his bulk through the narrow gap. Moments later the kitchen door opened.

'At your service, ma'am!'

'Thank you!'

She was shaking, but didn't know if it

14

was from cold, fury, or the disturbing closeness of this dream of a man.

'Now, hadn't you better get back to the job Mrs Kemp's paying you for?'

'Sure thing. See you later.'

For the rest of that day Janie was unable to concentrate. She dithered at the bank, unable to decide how much cash she would need.

At the supermarket checkout she stared in dismay at the best brand of coffee beans and a dozen packets of chocolate biscuits in her trolley. Where were the cornflakes and the sliced bread she'd meant to get, and why had she bought cream instead of skimmed milk, and expensive wine rather than the usual plonk?

She was off her trolley, she told herself, grinning ruefully, but she hadn't the nerve to admit to her absent-mindedness and put them all back. She'd look such a fool and Tracey, the checkout girl, who knew her well because Tracey's mum came in to do her cleaning once a week, would comment.

Tracey commented anyway.

'Having a house-warming?' she asked. 'It's today you move, isn't it?'

'Yes,' Janie said, unloading the biscuits.

She was about to tell Tracey about the removal company letting her down, then paused. Tracey would want to know every detail about the rescue, and Janie for some reason didn't want to have her exclaiming over it, telling her mum, and then Tracey's mum wanting her own account next time they met.

'Such a pity about your lovely old cottage, and Mrs Kemp's house, though that was only a hundred years old, wasn't it? Odd, I always thought, the two being so close together, yet lots of space all round.'

'The cottage was the original farmhouse, then they built a new one. When Mrs Kemp bought them, she wanted to knock the cottage down, but they wouldn't let her, so she sold it to Aunt Jane.'

'And now they're knocking both down just for a new industrial park,' Tracey said. 'Makes you think, doesn't it?'

'They could hardly have built round us.'

'You'll be better off in the flats.'

Janie wasn't so sure about the flat, but she'd had little choice. She'd had to find somewhere in a hurry, and the flat, a mere small two-room affair though it was, had been the best available. She was renting while looking for somewhere else to buy with the compensation she had received from the council when the cottage had been compulsorily purchased. At least it was on the ground floor, and she had a small patch of private garden.

She hurried back home. But it wouldn't be home for much longer, she thought sadly as she drove. It wouldn't exist in a couple of days. She'd sold some of Aunt Jane's furniture a week ago, the antiques had gone into store until Janie had a permanent home for them, and from that day it had been alien to her. Briskly, she told herself to stop regretting what couldn't be helped. There were more jobs to do. She still had the bedroom curtains to take down.

The van had gone, and so had Mrs Kemp's car. Janie felt a wave of relief sweep over her. She'd sensed Mrs Kemp's annoyance when her removal men had come to the rescue, and didn't want to hear any caustic comments. Mrs Kemp had a bitter tongue at times.

The older woman had bought a house in a village several miles away, but she hadn't given Janie the address. They had been no more than polite neighbours. Being the only houses in the lane they'd had to be. Janie had fed her cat when she'd been away, she had taken in parcels when Janie was at work, but nothing more. They moved in different circles. Mrs Kemp had her good works, bridge evenings and cocktail parties. Janie had her friends at the hospital and the health centre.

Janie made some tea. The men would be ages, no doubt. She took the mug into the sitting-room, kicked off her shoes, and sank on to the big settee, sipping slowly. She had loved it here, the place had so many memories, but it was a long drive into Bath, where she worked, especially at night. Maybe she ought to look for something there if she could afford it.

She was half asleep, and jumped when there was a sudden knock at the door. The men must be back already. Stumbling to her feet, she tripped over her shoes and dropped the mug. Tea splashed over the ancient carpet. As she cursed her clumsiness, hastily scooping up the two halves of the broken mug, another thing the wretched man would despise her for, she had time to be relieved she wasn't taking the carpet with her. Aunt Jane's money would stretch to new ones when she knew where she was going.

'You're back early,' she said, and the dark-haired one raised his eyebrows, then laughed.

'I thought you'd be pleased to see me.'

His tone was provocative, and Janie blushed as she saw him eyeing her dishevelled state.

'Would you like some tea?' she asked, more to divert his attention than because she wanted to prolong the business.

'No thanks, we'd prefer to get straight on. Tim has a date tonight. Everything's to go, I presume? Can you show us what there is?'

Janie had believed that all removal men drank copious amounts of tea. The ones who had brought her own things here and those who had packed Aunt Jane's antiques for storage had all seemed to stop for a cup between every trip to and from the van. But this way she'd be spared the chit-chat.

The two men worked silently, scarcely even talking to one another.

There were not even the usual, 'Your way a bit' or, 'Ready now' comments, but they worked well together, just the occasional word from the one whose name she didn't know. Tim was totally silent, and Janie found herself wondering how on earth he managed on a date if he was always so taciturn.

Very soon they were done, everything loaded. Janie came into the sitting-room to find them rolling up the carpet.

'I'm not taking that old thing,' she said quickly.

'This old thing is probably worth a few pounds. Kashmiri, I'd guess. What do you think, Tim?'

Tim nodded, and muttered something indistinguishable.

'Tim knows his carpets. You ought to take it. I — we can store it for you if it's a nuisance in your new place. Could arrange to sell it, if you like.'

'Of course, it would fetch more without mug handles caught in it,' the wretched man said, grinning, handing Janie a bit she'd missed.

She almost snatched it from him, and slung it into a corner of the room.

'The bulldozers can have it.'

He laughed. 'What's the address? Best if we have it, but we'll follow you, OK?'

Sooner than she'd imagined, Janie's furniture was set up in the new flat. It looked rather crowded now, but at least her own stuff made it feel more like home. She reached for her purse.

'Thanks a lot. What do I owe you?'

He didn't reply for a moment.

'Tell you what. I'll sell the carpet, and let you know whether we owe you, or the other way round. OK, Tim?'

Tim nodded.

'So long,' he said, and walked out.

'Aren't you going too?' Janie asked, a slight feeling of panic creeping into her mind.

Where was the nearest weapon? Had she unpacked her kitchen knives? She began to edge towards the door into the kitchen.

'I live just round the corner, only a

couple of minutes away, but I wondered if you had a Band-Aid?' he was now saying.

'Band-Aid?'

What was he talking about?

He held out his hand, and Janie could see a trickle of blood seeping from beneath a dirty strip of sticking plaster on his left wrist.

'You'd better let me wash that before it gets infected.'

Janie reached for her first-aid box.

'How did it happen?'

'I cut myself on your broken bit of mug. Wasn't expecting it.'

Janie felt horribly guilty.

'I'm sorry! I thought I'd picked it all up, really I did. But why is it still bleeding?'

'I knocked it again just now. I thought perhaps a nurse might be able to do something about it.'

'How did you know I'm a nurse?'

'My — Mrs Kemp mentioned it. After you'd gone back in your cottage.'

Janie frowned, tinglingly aware as she

remembered the feel of his body when he'd pulled her from the window. As she bathed the wound, put on some salve, and covered it, she couldn't help noticing how smooth and well-shaped his hands were, not at all rough as she'd imagined a removal man's hands to be.

'There, that should do. But change it once a day, until the cut closes.'

'Yes, nurse! Now, you won't want to bother cooking tonight. There's a good restaurant just round the corner. I'll nip home to have a shower, and call for you in half an hour.'

2

She had meant to refuse. She had tried to refuse. Janie still couldn't decide quite how she had come to agree to the astonishing invitation. But here she was, her hair swept up into a chic pleat, wearing her new dress. She'd bought the sleek, long-skirted blue silk dress last week, and had meant to save it for the birthday party of her friend, Mandy, at a posh restaurant in Bristol next month.

Instead, she'd now chosen to wear it in a small, intimate Italian restaurant, lit romantically with pink candles, having dinner with a man whose name she didn't know. And it was no excuse to say it had been the easiest to find in her cases of clothes. She'd opened three cases before she'd found it.

All she knew about the man sitting opposite her, in fact, was that he was handsome in a slightly foreign way, looked devastating in a dark grey suit, had an irresistible smile, and worked for some removal company. Now she came to think of it, the name hadn't been on the plain white van, which had disappeared anyway. He had called for her and they had walked the short distance to the restaurant. Janie supposed she was glad she hadn't had to ride in the van.

'Let's order. I can recommend the wild mushroom soup, and the chicken with tomatoes and prawns.'

Janie was happy to accept these suggestions. She'd never eaten here, but this man seemed to know it well. Several of the waiters had smiled at him as they were being shown to their table.

When they had ordered, and were drinking a smooth, fragrant white wine, he grinned.

'Perhaps we ought to introduce ourselves,' he said.

Had he read her mind?

'It's time to stop being incognito. I'm

Manuel Wickham.'

'Manuel? That's Spanish, isn't it?'

'I'm three-quarters Spanish. My mother and my father's mother were Spanish. We lived in Mexico when I was a child.'

So that explained the slight accent, the hint of American. Janie suddenly recalled Mrs Kemp calling him 'man'. Had she been using his name?

'Mrs Kemp, does she know?'

'Know what? That I was raised partly in Mexico?'

The way he lifted one eyebrow and his lopsided grin were doing wicked things to her. She would not allow herself to be beguiled by him. She hadn't time for a new relationship since she'd broken up with Robert, when he'd left to work in Australia, and she'd refused to abandon her own career to go with him. Janie forced herself to concentrate.

'No! She said something to you, called you Man. Is that your name, or a short form of it?'

'My — Mrs Kemp would never shorten it. I expect she was interrupted. But, yes, she does know my name.'

It seemed rather odd. Mrs Kemp was not the sort of woman to be on first name terms with workmen. Before Janie could ask more, get to the bottom of this, she was interrupted.

'Well, look who's here. Hello, Janie. Did the move go well? I'd have thought you'd have been too knackered to have a night on the town.'

Janie twisted round and glared at the man who'd tapped her on the shoulder. He was almost as tall as Manuel, but his eyes were too close together, and he had a permanent bad-tempered expression on his pale, slightly puffy face. He'd never ceased to torment her, jibing at her whenever they met, since she'd rejected his clumsy overtures years ago. She'd been sixteen and he, at more than twenty, had considered himself so much more sophisticated as well as being irresistible.

'Everything's fine, thank you,' she

replied curtly, and glanced at his companion.

She'd met Christine Harker, who worked for a local travel agent, several times, but the younger girl didn't acknowledge her, staring instead at Manuel with a hungry expression on her face.

'Won't you introduce us to your friend?' Brian asked.

'Manuel Wickham, this is Brian Cook and Christine Harker.'

'You must be new to the area,' Brian said. 'I thought I knew most of Janie's colleagues.'

Janie fumed. He was fishing for information, implying he knew her better than in fact he did, and at the same time hinting that no-one but a colleague would bother to take Janie out to dinner.

Brian laid his hand on one of the other chairs at their table, as if he was about to pull it out. Janie opened her mouth to tell him he wasn't wanted, and never mind that it would sound rude, and give him the wrong impression about her relationship with her companion, but Manuel spoke first.

'Quite new to the area,' he said in a cool voice. 'It was nice to meet you, but I think that's our waiter with our first course.'

Flustered, Brian glanced round. There was a waiter hovering behind him, but he didn't carry anything. He spoke to Brian.

'Your table is ready, sir. Over here, please.'

Brian glanced suspiciously at Manuel.

'Give Liz my regards,' he said to Janie. 'Your sister's become a very pretty girl.'

Reluctantly he turned and followed the waiter to a table at the far side of the room. The man came back to them.

'Sir?' the waiter asked. 'You want something?'

'Nothing more, thank you.'

Their hands met briefly, and Janie watched, disbelieving, as the waiter murmured his thanks and slipped something into his pocket.

'Did you call him over 'specially to get rid of Brian?' she asked.

'It seemed the most polite way. Better than telling him that his company was irritating, and superfluous.'

'But how did he know that was what you wanted? You didn't say anything at all to him!'

'Matteo is astute enough to understand that I would not want to have my evening with you ruined by impertinent intrusions. The Italians are a romantic race.'

Janie laughed.

'Whenever I want a waiter they ignore me.'

'That I find hard to believe, a lovely girl like you.'

Janie decided it was best to ignore this.

'But how did you know I wanted to get rid of him? He might have been a great friend.'

'If that's how you greet your friends, how do you treat your enemies?'

'He's neither,' she said swiftly.

Well, he wasn't, was he?

'He's a sort of distant connection. We're not related, not in any way.'

'Good, then we can forget him. Tell me about your work. Do you specialise? Which hospital do you work at?'

The next two hours sped by. It was only when they were walking back to her flat that Janie realised she knew nothing about Manuel, other than his tastes in films and music and holiday destinations. She didn't know where he lived, anything about his family, why he had left Mexico, and what brought him to live and work in this area. She felt annoyed, cheated. She wanted to know more. Had he been deliberately evasive?

At the entrance to the flat, which had its own doorway to the street, she turned to say good-night.

'I have enjoyed our evening, Janie, and really hope you will dine with me again soon.'

'I've enjoyed it, too. Thank you, and thank you as well for coming to my rescue today. I don't know what I'd have done without your help. And Tim's, of course.'

'Our pleasure. I'll contact you soon about the sale of the carpet. Now go in, and sleep well in your new home.'

He raised her hand to his lips and kissed it lightly. Janie gulped. No-one had ever done that to her before, and somehow it was exciting in a way very different from a more demanding embrace.

She turned to put her key in the door, and as it opened a voice could be heard, crying hysterically.

'Someone is here?' Manuel asked urgently, holding her arm and preventing her from running inside. 'Be careful.'

Janie shook her head.

'It's my sister, on the answerphone. What on earth's the matter?'

She ran into the living-room but as she reached the machine the call ended. All she had been able to hear was a frantic plea to ring back at once. Janie pressed the play button, and waited impatiently for the tape to rewind. She was vaguely aware that Manuel had followed her in and shut the outer door, but her concern for her sister overrode all other considerations. What had happened now?

At last the recorded message started.

'Janie, oh, Janie, are you there? I have to speak to you. It's desperate. I'm in real trouble, and he'll kill me when he finds out. Janie, if you're there please pick up the phone. I need you, now, and I'm so scared. Janie, ring me. I don't know what to do!'

The rest of the message consisted of a few words, interspersed with wild sobs, but so far as Janie could make them out they were mainly words like danger, afraid and murder.

As the message ended she turned to look at Manuel. He took her hand and led her over to the settee.

'Sit down, and tell me about your sister. Where is she, and how old?'

'I have to go to her! You heard her! I

34

must phone her.'

'In a moment. You must be calm, for her sake. Don't worry. I'll take you in my car. It's probably faster than yours. But tell me a little first. Who is it she's afraid of?'

Under his calm questioning Janie pulled herself together and tried to organise her thoughts.

'Liz is twenty, six years younger than me. She shares a flat north of Bristol with an old schoolfriend. She's out of jobs more often than in them, and has a knack of attracting rotten men.'

'They are violent towards her?'

'The last one was. I thought she had a new one now.'

'Ring her and find out. But try to stay calm.'

Janie nodded and punched in the number.

'Liz? It's all right, we'll come and help I only just got home. But what's the trouble?'

'Oh, Janie, thank goodness. It's Terry.'

'The new man? What's he done? Has he beaten you?'

'No, not yet. But he'll kill me when he finds out what I've done!'

She dissolved into tears and it was some time before Janie could get some sense out of her. Eventually, Liz swallowed her sobs and explained.

'I borrowed his car. He's away, so wasn't using it, and Steve, his flatmate, gave me the keys and said it would be OK. My car broke down and I had this new job, I didn't want to be late, as it might be a permanent one. And you've always nagged me to get a proper job!'

'What happened?' Janie asked, thinking of all sorts of disasters.

Why did Liz seem to attract trouble?

'On the way home, this flash car cut in front of me and I braked hard, and the car skidded, and, oh, Janie, I crashed into him, his car, I mean. And both of them, the cars, are write-offs.'

'Was anyone hurt?' Janie interrupted. 'Are you OK? Really not hurt?'

'Only scratches, from broken glass.

The other driver broke his arm, but the hospital said it was a simple fracture. But Terry will kill me!'

'It was an accident,' Janie tried to reassure her. 'And from what you say it sounds as though the other driver caused it. Surely Terry will understand.'

'You don't know how much he loves that car! He went berserk and threatened all sorts of things when some kid on a bike knocked his wing mirror crooked. If the car had been going, I think he'd have chased him, but the kid went down a narrow alleyway, and Terry couldn't catch him on foot.'

'Surely that's a bit excessive.'

'He's so proud of that car! There aren't many of them around, he says, and the other was an expensive one. It rolled right over.'

Janie felt helpless.

'Surely it's not so bad. No-one was seriously hurt, and the insurance will cover the damage to the cars.'

Liz began to sob again.

'That's the trouble. Terry's car wasn't

insured. He'd been meaning to send it off but he forgot. The other driver said he'd sue me for the damage, and loss of earnings, and injury and all sorts of other things I can't remember now. The police will prosecute me, too, but Terry will go ballistic! Janie, I'm so scared!'

'OK, calm down. Where's Terry now?'

'He's in London, at a friend's stag party. He won't be back until tomorrow, unless someone from the police, or Steve, his flatmate, managed to get in touch with him.'

'How did you find out about Terry not being insured?'

'When Steve came to collect the car. He told me then.'

'So he did know. But I don't understand. How did he collect it? Was it still possible to drive it?'

'No, but Steve has a repair garage. I rang him and he brought the breakdown truck. He said it would cost a lot to get anyone else, and we were causing an awful tailback.'

Janie groaned. What sort of a person was this Steve, who knew the car was uninsured and still allowed Liz to drive it?

Liz was crying again.

'Janie, it really wasn't my fault, but they'll all blame me, and the other driver said he'd sue me even though it was his fault. Can he do that? But anyway, if Terry finds me first I probably won't be alive to be sued!'

'Don't be silly. Look, we'll come and get you. You can come back here for a few days, out of his way, until we can sort it out. Terry won't know where you are. Pack a case, and we'll be there in less than an hour.'

She listened to Liz's sobs, now more of relief than fear, and eventually managed to end the call.

'I gathered some of that,' Manuel said. 'Tell me as we go. It'll be quicker if you come with me to get my car. But it won't take a moment to change into something more suitable for being cried over.'

Janie choked back a laugh. Liz was in plenty of trouble, but it would not help if her new silk dress was ruined. She nodded, and went into the bedroom, slipped out of the dress and dragged on jeans, a thick sweater, and trainers. Manuel was waiting by the door, her small evening bag in his hand.

'Is this enough? Do you have all you might need? Don't forget your keys.'

He really didn't live far away, just a couple of blocks. They hurried through the quiet streets, and he explained that he had a flat in one of the older Victorian houses, one which had not been demolished to build a small block of flats, like the one Janie lived in. She was too worried about Liz and her problems to take much notice of her surroundings, but she saw that his car was parked in a wide driveway. He handed her in and swiftly got it going.

It was low-slung, and comfortable, but Janie hardly noticed, she was too busy working out the best route to Liz's house once they reached Bristol.

Manuel seemed to know the way, and only asked for directions as they joined the Bristol bypass.

Janie had told him all she knew, all Liz had told her, and he had not tried to play down the gravity of the situation. She was grateful. False optimism would have grated. She didn't know herself how she could help Liz, but her sister had clearly once more attracted a man who could be violent, and at least she could protect her from his fury.

When Manuel pulled up outside an old, dilapidated house, Janie climbed out of the car.

'Wait, I'll come in with you, in case Terry is there.'

But before they had walked up the short path the door opened, and a distraught Liz almost fell out on to the step.

'Janie, I thought you'd never get here!'

Janie suppressed the retort that they'd done the journey in record time,

41

thanks to Manuel.

'Calm down, Liz. You're safe now. Where's your case?'

'Here it is,' a new voice said, and a girl Liz's age came out of the hall carrying a large holdall.

Manuel took it from her, put a protective arm about Liz, and began to lead her towards the car.

Janie turned to thank the girl.

'It's Rosa, isn't it? I remember you.'

'You won't tell Terry where I am?' Liz demanded, suddenly turning back, looking anxious again.

'I won't know where you are. I don't know Janie's new address,' Rosa said, casting her eyes upwards. 'Don't worry, Liz! You'll be safe while it's all sorted out. And I wouldn't tell that baboon, Terry Hughes, even if I did know.'

Liz looked doubtful, but responded to Manuel's gentle urgings and went towards the car again.

Janie glanced at Rosa, who shrugged.

'I'll ring you tomorrow?' Janie said quietly.

'Sure. She's so besotted, she won't tell you the truth,' Rosa whispered back. 'I work at the Crown Hotel. You can get me there during office hours.'

They didn't speak on the way home. Liz was in shock, and when she fell asleep Janie knew it was the best thing for her. At home, Liz staggered into the flat, meekly accepted a drink of hot milk and was almost immediately fast asleep in Janie's bed.

Manuel was in the sitting-room when Janie went back, idly looking through Janie's books which were piled on the floor.

'Thank you,' Janie said quietly. 'I don't know how to thank you.'

'No need. But let me know if there is anything more I can do. Where are you going to sleep?'

'The settee,' she said, indicating it. 'I've done it often enough before. That's why I bought such a big one.'

'Do you want to talk? I could do with a coffee.'

Janie sighed.

'So could I!'

She made a potful, tipped one of the packets of chocolate biscuits on a plate, and carried the tray back into the sitting-room. Manuel took it from her and put it on a small table, then he poured coffee into two mugs, stirred in sugar despite Janie's protest that she never had it, and added cream.

'I don't know if sweet coffee is as good as sweet tea,' he said, with that devastating smile, 'but it can't hurt you.'

'What will they do? The police, I mean, to Liz.'

She didn't pause to think it was odd for her to be asking him, who had lived in another country for most of his life, what the English police were likely to do about law breaking. Somehow he inspired confidence, and unlike some men didn't run away when trouble loomed. Trouble which had nothing to do with him, she reminded herself, once more feeling guilty.

'It depends on the circumstances, whether the accident was in any way her fault, due to dangerous driving or a car which was unroadworthy, for instance, or whether the other driver was to blame.'

'She said the other car cut in front of her, so surely he was responsible.'

'We'll soon know. They'll charge her with driving while uninsured, maybe taking it away if she didn't have permission to drive it, I guess. It could depend on how vindictive the boyfriend is. If he says she had permission to drive, she could get away with that, but from what she says he's not the type. I hope it will be just a fine.'

Janie groaned.

'And she has no money. As for Terry, from what she said, I suspect he'll be more concerned about his car than Liz. Why do some women always go for men who aren't in any way decent? She even had a fling with Brian when she was barely sixteen, and he was a dozen years older and anyone with half a brain can see he's mean and unreliable.'

Manuel grinned, but ignored this sidetracking.

'Does she exaggerate? Is she really so afraid of him?'

'She dramatises, she always has, but I think this was real.'

Suddenly it was all too much, and Janie covered her eyes as they filled with tears. When Manuel pulled her towards him and began stroking her hair she gave way, her pent-up anxieties overcoming her.

'I'm sorry,' she muttered into his shirt. 'I'll be OK in a minute.'

'You've been strong up to now for Liz. You have the right to relax a while. And don't worry about my shirt. It can stand a few tears.'

Janie sniffed, and laughter mingled with her sobs. She tried to push herself away, but found herself imprisoned in his arms.

'Relax, I'm comfortable, and I like holding you. Now, what can I do tomorrow?'

'Don't you have to work?' Janie asked.

It was dreadfully tempting to think she could rely on him, but she had to be strong.

'I can take a few days off. No problem.'

Guiltily, Janie wondered if his absence would cause other people to be let down in their removal plans.

'Can they spare you, your firm? Have they other men to cover for you?'

'I said, no problem. I'll do what I can to help, talk to the police, this other man's solicitor, if he has one, whatever.'

'It would be a help,' Janie admitted. 'I have a feeling I'll be fully occupied soothing Liz.'

'That's settled. I'll come round at nine. Will that be too early?'

'No, and thank you. I don't know why you should help us like this. You only met me this morning.'

'Yesterday morning. It's well after midnight. Now, don't worry, and try to sleep.'

47

He dropped a light kiss on her forehead and gently put her aside as he stood up.

'Lock the door after me. And don't worry.'

3

Janie was woken at half-past seven when Liz went through to the kitchen to make a cup of tea.

'I'm so afraid, I can't sleep,' Liz said, sniffing. 'What's going to happen? I'm sorry I woke you,' she added belatedly.

'I didn't sleep much either,' Janie told her, yawning. 'Make me a cup, too. I want to hear exactly what happened.'

An hour later Janie had heard the whole story from a tearful, still shocked, and horribly frightened Liz. At least, she thought she had disentangled the main facts from Liz's rambling, disjointed mixture of excuses and worries, but some things still puzzled her.

'Steve Bowcott will tell Terry what the other man was threatening,' Liz concluded.

'So Steve took the car away. Had the police been by then? Did they let him?'

'He got there first, and he said they wouldn't be interested, they'd want the road cleared. And the constable who took my name and address didn't seem to care.'

'You'll have to let the police know you're here,' she told her sister. 'Don't worry, they won't tell Terry. Do you want more toast? There's some left.'

Liz shook her head.

'No thanks. He'll expect me to pay for the car, though,' she said. 'And I'm overdrawn to my limit at the bank, and owe hundreds on my credit card.'

Janie suppressed a hot retort. It wouldn't help. She reflected grimly that she would no doubt be expected to bail her sister out of trouble, yet again. Half of the cash Aunt Jane had left her had already gone towards paying for Liz to have secretarial training, buying her a car, and contributing towards the deposit on her flat, not to mention many smaller loans when her sister had been unable to find a job. Their parents had suffered severe losses on some investments, and now lived on a very small pension, so could do little to help.

'You'll have to sell your car, leave the flat, and come to live with me until you get straight,' she decided. 'At least you won't have to pay rent, and there will be some sort of job you can do round here, even if it's stacking supermarket shelves. That will pay for your food, and you can save something.'

Liz began to protest that she didn't want to be away from all her friends in Bristol, but when Janie held up her hand, she subsided.

'You don't have much option, especially if you want to keep out of Terry's way.'

Liz shivered.

'He'll want to kill me.'

'Was his car totally wrecked? And how did you get off without more than bruises if it was?'

'I didn't follow what Steve said about the car when he took it away.'

'Did he have a good look at it then? Could he be sure?'

'He looked at it when he got it back to his workshop, and rang me. I'd been at the hospital. It was something about all the panels being dented, and it would be too expensive to find replacements. There aren't many that size, or something, or not many of his model were ever made. And the car wasn't worth spending on anyway, it had done too many miles.'

'That's the first cheerful thing I've heard. Why is Terry so attached to it?'

'It's unusual, I suppose. I don't know much about cars.'

'At least you didn't wreck this year's Porsche. What sort of car was the other one?'

Liz shook her head.

'I said, I can't tell them apart. But I haven't any money to pay for it, even if I did know. And even if they don't send me to prison, surely there'll be a huge fine.'

'They won't send you to prison. Don't be such a pessimist.'

'They will if I can't pay the fine, and

if the other driver sues.'

'He may not. It depends if it was his fault. He was trying it on, hoping to scare you, I expect.'

Janie struggled with her conscience. She had so loved owning her own house, and though she regretted losing the cottage, she had, in a way, begun looking forward to buying a house she could choose for herself. Now that prospect looked bleak. By the time she'd helped Liz, she'd be lucky to have enough left for a deposit, and on her salary as a nurse she wouldn't be able to afford much of a mortgage.

'Don't worry,' she said, suppressing a sigh. 'I've got the money from the house. I'll help you.'

Liz burst into tears of relief.

'Oh, Janie, I'm so afraid of Terry. I'll pay you back when I can.'

Not in a million years, Janie thought ruefully. Liz had been jealous, she knew, when Aunt Jane had left everything to her, but Liz hadn't been her godchild. Perhaps she saw this as her right. On the other hand she had been delicate as a child, over-indulged, their parents' favourite daughter.

While Janie had been rebellious and independent, Liz had been compliant, the good one. Yet Liz would never appeal to them for help, even if they could have afforded it. Was she afraid of destroying the image they had of her as a sweet little girl?

She sent Liz back to bed, telling her to try and sleep again now she knew the problem of money had been settled.

'You'll feel better by the afternoon. Then we can start to deal with it.'

Janie was sitting at the table, trying to work out how much she had in the bank, when the doorbell rang. She glanced at her watch. Manuel was early, it was barely half-past eight.

When she flung open the door, however, it was Brian standing on the step. He looked remarkably pleased with himself, and Janie frowned. She knew from previous experience that when Brian was in a complacent mood, it usually meant he was about to be unpleasant.

'This is a bit of a comedown after the cottage, isn't it?' he said, stepping inside before she could bar the way.

'I'm renting it while I look round for a house,' Janie told him, thinking that now she would probably be renting it for years to come.

He turned and grinned at her.

'That's good. It means we can split the proceeds.'

'What do you mean?'

'How about a coffee, Janie? Let's talk this over in a civilised manner.'

Before she could tell him to go, he had walked into the living-room.

'I know how much you got for the cottage, and how much cash Aunt Jane left you. We can sell her antiques at auction, and split the profits evenly,' Brian said.

Janie laughed. How stupid did he think she was?

'She was not your aunt and she didn't leave you anything, so you needn't think I'm going to hand over her money!'

'I was her nephew,' he began, but Janie, by now incandescent with fury, interrupted him.

'Your father married Aunt Jane's sister,' she said fiercely, 'and that doesn't make you any sort of relative of hers! Besides, she was free to leave her money to whomsoever she wanted.'

'But she did, Janie, and it wasn't to you.'

'What nonsense is this?'

'She made a new will.'

'What? I don't believe it!'

'It was sent to me a few days ago. You remember that old kitchen dresser you sold?'

Janie narrowed her eyes.

'Of course I do. What about it?'

'The will was stuck behind one of the drawers, and it so happened a friend of mine was in the shop you sold it to when they found it and passed it on to me. I'm going to take it to a solicitor today. Everything is left to me.'

Janie was frantically trying to remember. The old dresser would not have fitted in the flat, and she doubted if it would in any modern house, with fitted kitchens. It hadn't been worth a great deal, it was no antique, just a rather roughly-made deal dresser. Janie hadn't seen why the bulldozers should have it, though, when she could sell it for a few pounds. But she was certain she had taken all the drawers out and cleaned it thoroughly before she'd sold it to the dealer.

'You couldn't have a genuine will like that,' she said. 'You probably forged it.'

'Do you want to test that in the courts?'

Janie closed her eyes. Not another court case on top of Liz's. It was too much all at once.

'Come on, Janie, you know we'd both lose more to the lawyers than it's worth. I'm offering you a generous deal. Half the amount Aunt Jane left. We'll share, equally.'

'What about me?'

Janie swung round. Liz, wearing an oversized T-shirt as a nightdress, was standing in the bedroom doorway. Brian whistled admiringly.

'Liz! What a sight for sore eyes. So you're the mystery visitor. What are you doing here? You live in Bristol. Or you did when I met you at that New Year party.'

'Why do you want Janie's money?' Liz asked, and Janie saw that she was looking frightened again.

'Liz, Aunt Jane's will is nothing to do with you. Go back to bed and try to rest.'

'But you're planning to give him half your money! And you said you'd help me! There won't be enough for us all.'

'I'm not planning to give Brian anything,' Janie snapped.

Did everyone want her just for the money?

At that moment, Manuel appeared in the doorway.

'Sorry to barge in, but your front

door was open, and I wondered if you were OK.'

Janie felt an irrational stab of relief. He would sort it all out. Then she chided herself for being naïve. Manuel had been kind yesterday, but she barely knew him, and he had nothing to do with either Liz or Brian. They were her problems.

He was looking at Brian with a decidedly unfriendly expression on his face. Brian, glancing round nervously, began to edge towards the door.

'That's all I have to say, Janie. I'll be off now. Think it over, and I'll see you tomorrow after I've consulted my solicitor.'

He sidled out of the door, scurrying as Manuel followed him into the tiny hallway. Despite her worries, Janie was amused. Then the front door slammed and Manuel came back into the room. Before he could speak, Liz had burst into angry speech.

'Janie, it's not fair! You promised to help me, and now you're suggesting sharing it with him!'

'Liz, I didn't! That was his suggestion! If you're not going to sleep, go and get dressed while I make some coffee for us all. Manuel, have you had breakfast?'

'Yes, but I'll have coffee, please. Now, what is all this?' he asked, following her into the kitchen while Liz hovered in the doorway. 'What was that man doing here? Was he bothering you?'

'You could say that!'

Janie filled the kettle and began to spoon coffee into the cafetiere.

'He claims he found another will, and that Aunt Jane left everything to him.'

'Is it likely? Was he related to her?'

'No, but his father married Aunt Jane's sister, so he knew her. She always said he was the most obnoxious little brat.'

He sat on one of the chairs by the kitchen table and absentmindedly began to nibble a piece of cold toast.

'So it's highly unlikely she'd favour him.'

'No. She never liked him.'

'Is it possible he had some hold over her?'

Janie shook her head.

'Of course not! She lived a blameless life. There were no scandals, nothing like that.'

'Nor connected with anyone else she might want to protect?'

'She had no relatives.'

Liz laughed suddenly.

'There was only you yourself, Janie.'

'That's ridiculous! And for heaven's sake go and get dressed!'

Liz flounced off, muttering. Manuel ignored her.

'Do you believe he could have a paper of some sort? A letter, perhaps, if not a will?'

'If he has, it must be a fake. But it would be expensive to try and prove it in the courts.'

'Which he knows, and is trying to con you into giving up your inheritance. And Liz? What had you promised her?'

'Well, to help her, of course. Manuel, what else can I do? I'm older, I have the money to help and I feel responsible for her!'

'You could let her grow up! That would be real help. She'll never become a responsible adult while she has you to come to her rescue. It was idiotic of her to take the car.'

'Perhaps. And I agree with you, as it happens. But it's too late now to wish she hadn't,' Janie interrupted.

Manuel nodded.

'OK, but she was criminally foolish to drive without insurance.'

'She didn't know about that! Why should she? If a friend lent you a car when you were desperate, would you insult him by asking if the insurance had been paid?'

'It would depend on how much I trusted my friend. I doubt ignorance will save her. And when did she find out?'

'When this man, Steve, came to take away the car and he told her.'

'And he was the one who let her drive it, knowing that? Wasn't that irresponsible of him?'

'Yes, of course it was.'

'Where is the car now?'

'Apparently Steve repairs cars, so it's in his workshop somewhere in Bristol.'

'Didn't the police want to examine it?'

'I understand not. Surely, as no-one was seriously hurt, they wouldn't bother.'

'It depends on whether they charge Liz with careless driving, I suppose. If they do, they may want to see if the car was roadworthy before they throw other charges at her.'

Janie groaned.

'I was hoping Steve had got it wrong, and perhaps Terry had sorted the insurance after all.'

'That's still possible, though I suspect unlikely, from what I've heard.'

'I agree, knowing the sort of people Liz gets mixed up with. But that's not her fault.'

'Of course it is. She ought to have more sense. She looks the irresponsible sort who'd trust anyone she met without a second thought.'

'As I did you!' Janie reminded him. 'Was I irresponsible, too? Letting you take away my furniture? And a carpet you said was valuable? Which you still have, incidentally.'

'That was different. You were desperate and I'm not a crook like these so-called friends of hers.'

'You don't know that.'

'Not for sure. But he was probably driving dangerously. You shouldn't have to bail her out. None of that's your responsibility.'

'She's my sister!'

'She's her own person, Janie. I didn't think you were a fool, but I'm beginning to alter my opinion,' he said, standing up. 'Let her sort out her own messes. She's quite old enough. She doesn't need nannying.'

She turned away, fighting down her anger at his lack of sympathy for her sister. Deep down, Janie knew he was right, but she wouldn't admit it.

'Then perhaps you'd better go.'

She forced herself to look at him.

'I was grateful for your help, but the fact you helped me yesterday doesn't give you the right to interfere with my life.'

He gazed at her for a long moment, and then swung on his heel and left the flat. Janie, trembling, closed her eyes and waited for the door to crash home, but he closed it gently, and she thought that showed more implacable anger than if he'd slammed it hard.

Liz came into the kitchen.

'Yum, that coffee smells good. We can only ever afford the cheapest instant. Where's Manuel? He's rather dishy, isn't he? Where did you find him?'

'He's gone,' Janie said shortly. 'He helped me move my furniture yesterday, and was still here when you phoned. That's all.'

She saw no reason to tell Liz they'd

been out to dinner together. That was over.

'I thought he was going to help me sort things out, talk to the police and so on.'

'Well, he's not, not now.'

Janie thought of something which had puzzled her earlier.

'Brian said you were at the same New Year party. I didn't know you were still in touch with him.'

'I'm not, but he knows people in Bristol, too. It was where I met Terry.'

'Brian knows Terry?'

Janie frowned. She didn't like the sound of this.

'I don't know. There were dozens of people there. What does it matter anyway?'

'They sound the same sort of people, that's all.'

'You never did like my friends!'

Liz appeared to have recovered her composure, and Janie could feel her own temper rising. It had always been the same. Liz attracted trouble, but as

66

soon as she had passed on the mess to someone else, she reverted to her usual cheerful, uncaring self.

As a child, their parents had always come to the rescue, but now they were living in Malta, Janie had taken their place, just there to pick up the pieces and make it all better for her little sister.

She was highly tempted to wash her hands of Liz's problems. Then she rejected the thought. Whatever happened, she couldn't do that.

'I'd better ring the police and tell them where you are, or they'll think you've absconded,' she said wearily. 'What's their number?'

For a wonder, Liz had it written down in her diary, and Janie was soon talking to the duty sergeant.

'She'll be here when you want her, officer, but please understand, she's terrified of Terry Hughes, the man whose car she wrecked. Please don't tell him or Steve Bowcott where she is. Hughes can be violent, and she doesn't feel safe at home. What else do I have to do?'

Liz was flicking through a magazine.

'Don't you have anything but these nursing things?' she asked when Janie put down the phone. 'They're boring.'

'Just be thankful you're not in intensive care, depending on nurses, and that the man you ran into wasn't killed.'

'Well, I'm not and he wasn't. Stop being such a wet blanket.'

Janie gritted her teeth and tried to speak calmly.

'The police will want to talk to you soon, the sergeant said. And he wants to know the address of Steve's workshop.'

'Why? It's nothing to do with them.'

'Of course it is! They probably want to see the car.'

'It was none of it my fault! Terry should have insured the car, and if that idiot hadn't swerved in front of me, I wouldn't have crashed.'

'The address, Liz!'

Reluctantly Liz told her and Janie relayed the information to the police as Liz stormed out of the room, saying she had had enough of being blamed and questioned and harassed.

Janie could tolerate no more either. She followed Liz into the bedroom.

'I'm going out. Don't let anybody into the flat, don't even answer the door, and don't answer the phone. You'd better stay in the bedroom or the kitchen, out of sight. Terry might find out about me and come here after you,' she added, seeing Liz about to refuse.

'Oh, all right, but he can't know your new address, even if he finds out I have a sister.'

'I wouldn't be too sure he couldn't find out. He may know Brian.'

'But he can't know Brian is a sort of cousin.'

Janie prayed for patience, and took her bag. She meant to visit the dealer who had bought her old dresser, and try to discover the truth of what Brian had said. She couldn't believe Aunt

Jane would have left anything to him. She'd always said what an obnoxious little boy he'd been, and an even worse man, but she had to check it out before she defied him to do his worst.

The shop, no more than a series of ancient sheds and lean-tos, was in a side street, and crammed full of old, and mainly tatty furniture. The elderly man in charge greeted her without enthusiasm and waved his hand.

'Look round, dear, and if there's anything you like, I'll be in me office at the back.'

'I don't want to buy anything. I sold you a dresser a week ago, and I heard some papers had been found in it. Is that true?'

He shrugged.

'There was a bit of a fuss, but I don't know no details. You'll have to come back when the boss is here.'

'When will that be?'

'How should I know? He don't tell me where he goes.'

'Is there anyone else here? A

secretary, someone to answer the phone, make appointments, keep the books?'

It was a forlorn hope, but to her surprise he gestured to a house across the road.

'You could try his missus. She'll be back from shopping by now.'

Janie thanked him and crossed the road. After several rings on the bell which went unanswered, probably because of the volume of the TV in the front room, she knocked loudly on the thin panels of the door. A raucous voice answered.

'I'm coming, don't knock the door down!'

The door opened and a wizened little woman peered out.

'What is it?'

Janie explained again, and to her dismay saw the woman beginning to nod.

'Yes, there was something. Bert said. A long envelope, with papers inside. But I didn't see it, an' I don't know what was in it.'

'Who found it?' she asked.

'Can't say. But Bert said it had some name on it. And he said he knew the feller, so he give him a bell, and the chap come over.'

She could tell Janie no more, and Janie retreated to a nearby coffee shop to think about it. It proved nothing, she realised. The woman hadn't seen the discovery, if there had been one, and Janie was positive there had been no envelope in the dresser.

It could have been planted, by Brian or one of his dubious acquaintances. And even if Bert had actually seen the envelope being found, she would continue to disbelieve it was genuine.

How could she discover who the man was who had found it, or was supposed to have done so?

She was pondering this question when someone sat down opposite her. Looking up, she saw Christine Harker, glaring at her with undisguised hostility.

Janie stared back. They'd never been

friends, so why had Christine bothered to join her? There were plenty of empty tables.

'What were you doing at Bert's?' the girl asked.

'Is it any of your business?'

'Might be. I was walking past and saw you there nosing about. I wondered if you were trying to check up on Brian and me. But you won't. The will's the real thing, properly written and witnessed. The cottage belongs to Brian by rights.'

'The cottage won't be there tomorrow.'

'No, but Brian would have put up more of a fight, got bigger compensation from the council. You've cheated him of that, but you won't get away with it.'

4

On the way back home, Janie was thinking hard. Could it have been Christine who had discovered the will, or pretended to? The fake will, she hastily amended, since she could not believe that Aunt Jane would have changed her mind, and left all her property to Brian, a man she detested.

She had to speak to Bert. She swung round and went back to the sale room, but he was still not there, and the elderly man told her with some relish that he wasn't likely to be back until late that night.

'House clearance,' he told her. 'Try again tomorrow.'

There was nothing more she could do here, and plenty that needed doing at home, telephone calls to make to Rosa and to find a solicitor to help Liz.

She began to walk slowly back to the

flat. Surely Liz could get legal aid? Maybe she ought to consult people who knew. Manuel had appeared to know what to do, she thought, yet why should a man who had lived most of his life elsewhere, in another country, and worked for a removal company, know about such matters?

Firmly she dismissed thoughts of him from her mind. That was over. He'd been helpful, and she'd enjoyed her evening with him, but he had no right to criticise her sister, even if in her heart she agreed with what he'd said. She couldn't abandon Liz, though it meant giving up her own dreams of a home she owned — a home she owned if Brian's will proved to be false.

That was something else she needed to deal with. She swung round again, and went back to the office of the solicitor who had drawn up Aunt Jane's will and dealt with the sale of the cottage. He'd tell her what to do.

He was out, but she made an appointment to see him the following day, and finally managed to go back home before she thought of other things which had to be done.

Liz was talking on the phone, and waved to Janie as she entered the sitting-room.

'Hi.'

'Who's that?' Janie demanded. 'I said not to answer the phone.'

'It's OK. I rang Rosa. She says Terry got back early this morning, had a lift straight after the party ended in the small hours, and as soon as he heard about the car he was banging on the door of the flat, waking up all the neighbours. Rosa had to let him search the whole flat before he'd believe I wasn't there. And he went round talking to the people in the flat next to us.'

'Let me talk to her.'

Reluctantly Liz handed over the receiver.

'Go and make some sandwiches for lunch, Liz.'

Liz pouted, but went into the

kitchen. Janie closed the door after her, then spoke quietly into the telephone.

'Now, Rosa, it's me, Janie. Is Terry really dangerous?'

'I think he could be,' Rosa said seriously. 'He almost broke our door down, he was so mad with rage. But he at least had the sense not to start on me. I told him Liz was in hospital.'

Janie groaned.

'I hope he doesn't cause too much trouble! We have enough violent patients without him, too!'

'I know, and I'm sorry, but at least they won't let him in. It seemed the best way to stall him. I didn't say which hospital, and it'll take him a couple of days to go to all of them and find out she isn't in any, I hope. By then he might have calmed down. Liz didn't sound too scared.'

'You know my sister! But some people know she isn't in hospital. Terry's flatmate, I suppose, since she rang his place and this man took away the car.'

'If he comes back to argue I'll say she had a relapse and went back for observation.'

Janie rang off.

Liz came back in with sandwiches, and afterwards Janie made an appointment for them to talk to someone at the Citizens' Advice Bureau later that afternoon. On the way, she called again at the second-hand shop, but Bert had still not appeared.

Later, reassured that Liz would have proper legal advice if she were prosecuted, they stopped for tea and scones at a small café in the town centre, then shopped for food and strolled home. They were both tired, and after a couple of hours watching programmes that held not the slightest interest for them, switched off the television and went to bed.

This time Liz offered to sleep on the settee, and Janie was so exhausted after her move and the problems of the day she didn't protest, but went thankfully to her own comfortable bed.

She slept late, and woke with a start. As she realised it was someone knocking on the front door which had disturbed her, she dragged on her robe and glanced at her bedside clock. It was after eight.

Liz, her hair tangled and her eyes wide with fright, rushed into the bedroom.

'It's Terry! It must be! Janie, what shall we do?'

'Stand by the phone, ready to phone the police,' Janie said, trying to stay calm.

'Who is it?' she demanded, not opening the door.

'Manuel. Are you ever going to let me in?'

He sounded coldly furious. Janie frowned. She hadn't expected to see him again, so what could he want? Cautiously she slipped on the chain and opened the door, and her heart gave a sudden lurch. He was dressed in black jeans and a thin white sweater which emphasised his dark good looks. He looked more incredibly handsome than she recalled.

'What do you want?' she asked.

'To talk, in a civilised fashion.'

'We thought it might be Terry,' Janie explained when she had removed the chain and let Manuel in.

'So he knows where you are, does he?' Manuel said, turning angrily towards Liz, who cowered away from him. 'I suppose you rang him to tell him.'

'No, of course I didn't!' Liz protested.

'But he knows something and I want to know how!'

'Look, calm down!' Janie said. 'You woke us up, and we can't talk like this. You know where the kitchen is, Manuel. How about making a pot of coffee while I have a shower?'

Under the shower, Janie tried to work out what Manuel meant by his angry words. Terry couldn't know where Liz was, for, if he did, surely he would have appeared by now. Yet Manuel had implied that Terry knew something. What? And how was Manuel involved?

He had brewed coffee, and a pile of toast awaited them when she joined them in the kitchen.

'Let's eat first,' he said, but he didn't smile and his tone was grim.

Janie had no appetite, but with his stern gaze on her she didn't feel like arguing, so she buttered a slice and began to nibble at it. Liz, for once remarkably brisk, joined them, but they all ate in silence.

'I can't stand this any more!' Liz suddenly exclaimed. 'What's the matter with you?'

Manuel pulled a crumpled sheet of paper, protected by a polythene bag, from his pocket and threw it down before them. It was damp, splattered with drops of red paint, and the crudely-printed capitals, done with a black marker pen, had run so that it was difficult to read.

'Don't get in my way or you'll regret it,' Manuel recited, his voice expressionless.

'Who did this? When did you find it?' Janie asked.

'It would be more appropriate to ask where. It was on the windscreen of my car this morning, where I normally park in the driveway of my house. My car had had all the wheels removed, the bodywork scored with obscenities, and red paint thrown all over the windows. They obviously came prepared. All nice quiet methods of vandalism which wouldn't have disturbed anyone at dead of night.'

'Oh, no! But who? Why are you accusing us?' Liz asked.

'I don't accuse you of anything except crass stupidity for letting that vicious brute of a boyfriend know where you are, and who helped you.'

It took time, but eventually Manuel accepted that neither of them had had any contact with Terry or let him know anything about Manuel's help.

'We didn't even tell Rosa where we were,' Liz said earnestly.

Manuel was looking less grim now.

'The only possible way is for someone who saw me fetching Liz away from her flat, and took my licence number. I suppose there are ways of tracing the owners, even though the information is not supposed to be given out.'

'Terry knew a couple of policemen,' Liz said slowly. 'He said one of them owed him a favour. I don't know what it was, but I expect he could find out.'

'If he's crooked, but I imagine most of Terry's friends are,' Janie said bitterly. 'Manuel, you were so good to us both, and I'm so sorry you've been attacked like this. It's so unfair!'

He smiled, for the first time that morning.

'Pure bad luck for someone to notice my car number. It must have been one of your neighbours, Liz. Any ideas?'

She shook her head.

'No, but there are a couple of elderly

women in one of the flats nearby who are always complaining that we make too much noise, and have too many visitors with noisy cars and bikes.'

'Have they done any more than complain to you?' Janie asked, wondering what sort of life Liz had been leading.

'They've called the police once or twice when we've had parties. Maybe they were snooping, taking car numbers as a hobby. If Terry talked to them they'd have told him.'

'Especially if he claimed to be from the police, or an environmental health officer from the council,' Janie suggested. 'Rosa said he talked to some of the neighbours, and it sounds like the sort of trick he'd pull. Manuel, you must let me pay for the damage to be put right,' she added, wondering how much in debt she would be by the time this was over.

She was by now resigned to losing all her inheritance one way or another.

'My insurance will pay, Janie. But

now I have my own quarrel with this villain. So tell me what has happened. You have contacted the police and a solicitor, I hope.'

Janie gasped and looked at her watch.

'Help, that reminds me! I have to see my solicitor in ten minutes! Manuel, will you stay here with Liz, please? I don't want to leave her alone.'

'Sure. Go on, I'll stay.'

Janie ran all the way, and arrived only five minutes late. She panted into the reception area, and gasped out apologies.

'It's all right. Mr Simpson has been held up with another client, but he phoned in to say he'll be here in ten minutes. Can I get you a coffee?'

An hour later she was on her way back home, having been reassured that Mr Simpson thought it most unlikely that his late client would have changed her mind about her will, or used another solicitor to draw one up.

'She did all her legal business through the firm, first with my uncle, and when he retired, with me. I shall subject this other one to the closest scrutiny. And I will go and see the man who runs the second-hand furniture business, and see what light he can throw upon the supposed finding of it. Tell Mr Cook to have his solicitor contact me.'

The opportunity for that came sooner than Janie had expected. At the flat she met Brian approaching from the opposite direction.

'Not back at work yet?' he asked her. 'I thought nurses worked all the time, they are so valuable they can't be spared.'

Janie fitted her key into the lock.

'If it's any business of yours, I took some of my holiday for moving. I'm entitled to that just as much as other people are. My solicitor, Mr Simpson, wants to speak to yours,' she added over her shoulder.

She opened the door and went inside, but before she could close it Brian had his foot in the doorway.

'Come on, Janie, you don't want to lose everything to the lawyers, do you? I made you a good offer, and if you agree I'll forget about this other will, which I think is generous of me. Why don't you share it, like I suggested, then we'll both be happy? If you don't, either I'll get the lot, or the lawyers will.'

'Go away, and get your foot out of the door!' Janie shouted at him.

Her nerves were beginning to disintegrate, she thought wildly. Too much was happening, too quickly.

'Janie, what's the matter?'

It was Manuel, and Janie turned to him.

'Please will you get rid of this — this bloodsucker!'

Brian had stepped back.

'Oh, I see, the boyfriend's moved in, has he? Tell him you won't have any money at all, so if that's what he's after he'd better have second thoughts. All right, old chap, I'm going. But you'll hear from me soon, Janie.'

He backed away, and Janie caught at

Manuel's clenched hand.

'Let him go,' she urged, 'he's not worth hitting.'

Manuel glanced down at her, and Janie quickly let go of his hand.

'Why do you two girls attract trouble?'

5

'We'll go and see this second-hand dealer,' Manuel said. 'Did you try him today when you were in town?'

'No, I was anxious to get back here.'

'Can I come, too?' Liz asked. 'I don't want to stay here by myself. I'm too scared.'

'I think it best you do stay here,' Manuel told her. 'Just think, if Terry is watching me, he may expect me to lead him to you.'

'But if he is, and sees you here, surely leaving Liz on her own is risky?' Janie said, worried.

'Does he know you're her sister?'

Janie shook her head.

'I've never met him. Liz, does he know about me? Where I live, anything like that?'

'No, you were never mentioned. I've only known him a few weeks. We

89

haven't got around to exchanging family histories! But I don't want to stay here on my own!'

'Keep away from the windows, don't answer the door or the phone, and we'll be back in less than an hour, unless you'd like me to go on my own to the dealer?' he added, turning to Jane.

'No, I'd better come. You wouldn't recognise the dresser.'

Liz protested, but Manuel patiently reassured her.

'He doesn't know Janie, and you don't really look like her, you're much darker and not so tall. Even if he sees Janie and me together why should he associate you with us? He may know me, if he was watching my flat and followed me here, but there aren't many places for him to hide, to watch this flat, and for all he knows Janie might be just a girlfriend.'

Janie wasn't sure what to make of the 'just', then she chided herself for being silly. She wasn't his girlfriend in any sense. Not that she'd have objected, though. Then she shrugged off the idea. She was off men since Robert, and such a good-looking man as Manuel probably had girls lining up for him.

'I imagine he'd get out of the area fast, after what he did to Manuel's car. From the way this letter's splattered I'd expect there to be some paint on his clothes. There's no reason for him to know or even suspect you're here. For all he knows, Manuel could have just taken you to a friend's house, in Bristol or anywhere. If whoever took the car number told him I was there, I could have been anyone.'

'They could have described you to him. And the chances are you live near Manuel,' Liz insisted.

Janie nodded.

'That's true, but we're speculating, and arguing isn't getting us anywhere. You can't stay in hiding for ever. Manuel, have you told the police about the damage to your car?'

'Yes, and they will be coming round

to inspect it, and I have to give them this note.'

'Then you have to go back home soon,' Janie said, and was surprised at the dismay she felt.

Liz's anxiety was beginning to affect her nerves.

'So the sooner we get moving the better. You'll be fine, Liz, and we won't be long. Come on, Janie.'

At the dealer's they found a big, beefy man supervising the unloading of a small van, not unlike the one Manuel and Tim had used for Janie's furniture. He was cursing two weedy-looking youths who didn't look strong enough to carry the big, old-fashioned wardrobe, shouting instructions at them as they manoeuvred it into place near the doorway.

When they turned to fetch the next item Manuel stepped in front of him and prevented him from leaving the shop.

'Are you Bert?'

'What if I am? What do you want?'

'I sold you an old dresser last week,' Janie cut in. 'I heard some papers had been found in it, and I wondered if that was true.'

'Look, dearie, I buy and sell lots of stuff. How can you expect me to remember every stupid piece?'

'So you don't remember these papers being found? Surely that would have been rather unusual?'

'They might have been. I'm not responsible for what gets left behind in drawers, we get all sorts of rubbish people have forgotten. But if you want them back, you'll have to pay me. What I bought from you I paid for.'

'But you don't have them. You sent them to the person whose name was on the envelope,' Manuel said, pulling out his wallet.

Bert glanced up at him from suddenly narrowed eyes.

'In an envelope, you say?'

'So I was told.'

'I do recall an envelope being found.

But you said papers. That's not an envelope.'

Janie tried to control her temper.

'Did you find them?'

Manuel rustled a couple of ten pound notes together, and Bert glanced at him, then smiled at Janie.

'No, luv. Someone who was looking round the shop said they'd found them. A girl, pretty little thing, said they'd been stuck at the back of a drawer and it hadn't closed properly, so she'd pulled it right out and found this envelope.'

'That's not possible,' Janie said. 'I had all the drawers out before you collected it, and there was nothing there then. I'd swear to that.'

'Where is the dresser?' Manuel asked. 'I'll have a look.'

'Now that you can't do. I sold it yesterday, cash, and I don't know the woman who bought it, but she took it away with her. She had a van like mine, full of stuff it was. I think she was another dealer, probably from Bristol or

Cardiff, hoping to do it up and make a few bob.'

'If you see her again, let Miss Tempest know who she is, please,' Manuel said, offering Bert the two ten pound notes.

He grasped Janie by the arm and hustled her outside.

'Well, he didn't admit to finding any papers, so it looks as though Brian's friend, Christine, planted it, if what we suspect is correct. She could be described as a pretty little thing, when she's not scowling.'

'But we are no further forward. What shall we do?' Janie asked.

'Wait until Brian's solicitor produces the will. Now I will see you home, make sure Liz is all right, and I must meet the police.'

'I'm so sorry about your car,' Janie said, sighing. 'If you want to borrow mine while it's being repaired, I'd feel a bit happier. I don't need it until I go back to work next Monday.'

'Thanks, Janie, but I'll hire one. I

can't leave you without a car.'

'You'll let us know what the police say?'

'Of course.'

'Come round for supper tonight.'

'Thank you, but I have to go to see someone. I'll phone, and I'd better give you my mobile number. Phone me if anything happens. But take care, and try to persuade Liz to be sensible.'

Janie felt deflated. She'd come to rely on Manuel's support. That was all, she tried to convince herself, but innate honesty made her admit that it was Manuel she wanted to be with.

* * *

By the time Sunday came, Janie was feeling ready to strangle Liz. Manuel had rung once on Thursday afternoon to say the police would be questioning Terry, but they heard no more. Janie feared he was getting tired of them. Liz had spells when she fretted about what would happen to her, whether she would have to pay an enormous fine, or lose her licence, or even go to prison, and then seemed to shrug it off and forget all about it when she recalled Janie's promises of help.

In that mood she complained that she was already in prison, and why couldn't she go out to get some fresh air, or do some shopping, or find a hairdresser to cut her hair.

Janie could stand the strain no longer, and suggested they drove out into the country for lunch.

'We'll head eastwards, away from Bristol, and find a small pub in the country.'

By the time they got back home they were both feeling more cheerful. The sun had emerged, the pub they found had delicious food, and on the way home they had called in at a garden centre for Janie to buy some house-plants.

'I miss the garden at the cottage,' she explained. 'I'd only just got used to having one, then it's snatched away from me by the council.'

'That was tough,' Liz agreed. 'Janie, what am I to do? Can I really come and live with you?'

Janie sighed inwardly.

'Let's see what happens, whether the police are going to prosecute you, whether Terry calms down.'

Liz shuddered.

'I don't want to see him ever again.'

Janie was thinking that she would have to find a larger flat if Liz did have to join her. They would need two bedrooms, for she was determined she would not share with her sister, and they could not continue to use the settee.

'I have to leave at the crack of dawn or before, in the morning. I'm on the early shift,' she said. 'I'd better sleep on the settee tonight and then I won't disturb you.'

Liz frowned.

'Does that mean you'll want to go to bed early? There's a programme on telly I wanted to watch.'

'You can take it into the bedroom, and yes, Liz, I must go to bed early. If I'm the one earning, then I need my sleep!'

Liz flounced out of the kitchen where they'd been eating supper.

'Then I'll go to bed now,' she said. 'I know I'm being a nuisance, but I'll keep out of your way.'

As she drove to work through the lanes the next morning, yawning, Janie thought ruefully that Liz's idea of keeping out of her way was to creep ostentatiously through the sitting-room several times during the evening, and come in while Janie was dressing to beg her not to go to work, for she'd be afraid to stay on her own.

'Ring Manuel's mobile if you're frightened,' Janie said briskly. 'Don't ring me at the hospital. You know I can't answer personal calls. But leave the curtains drawn and don't let anyone know you're here.'

She felt mean, but she hoped Liz would be sensible and keep out of sight.

As they had heard nothing more perhaps Terry's fury had been spent by the damage done to Manuel's car, and he would have other concerns. Perhaps the police had warned him. He might even be in trouble for not insuring his car.

There was little time to think, she was so busy all day. It was getting dark by the time she arrived back home, and she was looking forward to a soak in the bath and a glass of wine, then another early night when she might be allowed to sleep.

As she opened the door she heard voices. Apprehensive, she almost ran into the sitting-room, to find Liz sitting on the settee, and Manuel standing beside her. The relief, and the surge of joy she felt on seeing him, made her dizzy for a moment. Liz, seeing her, jumped to her feet.

'Janie, the solicitor rang. He wants you to go and see him when you can.'

'I thought you weren't going to answer the phone.'

'I didn't!' Liz was indignant. 'He left a message on the machine. I listened to that.'

'Oh, of course. Sorry. Nothing else has happened?'

'No, it's been deadly boring until Manuel came. Are you going down now? You'll have time before he closes.'

Janie groaned. She was exhausted and had no wish to go out again.

'I suppose I'd better. I'll change out of my uniform first.'

'I'll walk down with you,' Manuel offered. 'It will be as quick as trying to park. Liz can cook you a meal while we're out.'

Liz seemed about to protest, but Manuel smiled at her and she closed her mouth, nodded, and went reluctantly into the kitchen. Janie suppressed a grin. No-one else had ever been able to persuade Liz to help around the house. She existed on microwave meals and takeaways, or things on toast, Janie suspected. She was well aware of what her sister was like!

'Can your car be repaired?' she asked as they set off.

'Yes, but it will take time.'

'Terry shouldn't be allowed to get away with it!'

'He won't, don't worry. There are other ways of making him sorry for attacking me.'

Janie glanced up at him. His tone was grim, and she shivered. She would not like to get on the wrong side of him, she thought suddenly. He looked and sounded dangerous.

At the solicitor's office they were asked to wait, and then a junior clerk came out to usher them into a small anteroom.

'Mr Simpson is with a client, but he said to show you this when you came in, and to ask if you know either of the witnesses.'

She handed over a thin folder, and Janie opened it to find a photocopy of a simple will form, the kind that could be bought in stationery shops. She read the short document, a will dated just a few days before Aunt Jane died, leaving all her possessions to Brian Cook.

'Is this legal?' she asked the clerk.

'It could be. It's simple, but it would be accepted, if it is properly signed and witnessed, and isn't forged.'

Janie looked at the signatures. They were difficult to read, but eventually she made them out.

'One looks like Frank Jones. He used to do the garden for Aunt Jane, but he died last year.'

'So we can't ask him about it,' the clerk said. 'What about the other one? Do you know who that is?'

'I'm not sure. It's such untidy writing. It looks like Teresa Henny, but I don't know anyone of that name.'

'Let me see,' Manuel said, and took the paper from Janie. 'It's Kemp, not Henny.'

'Are you sure? Aunt Jane's neighbour? But I don't understand! If she knew Aunt Jane had left everything to Brian, why didn't she say something when I moved into the cottage?'

'She need not have known. The wording could have been covered so that the witnesses couldn't read it,' the clerk explained. 'All they have to do is sign that they witnessed the signature of the person making the will.'

'And I don't have her new address,' Janie said. 'Can you find out? She'd have arranged for her mail to be redirected, so maybe the Post Office will tell you.'

'That's no problem. But if the will and the signatures were forged it was likely they'd choose people who couldn't contradict it. But not clever enough. There are ways we can check up.'

Janie suddenly clapped her hand to her head.

'I'm more exhausted than I thought! Manuel, you'd know the new address. You helped to move Mrs Kemp's furniture.'

'That's not necessary. This is nothing like Teresa Kemp's signature,' Manuel said quietly. 'Her writing is much bigger, flamboyant.'

'How do you know? Did you see it on a letter to your removal company?' Janie asked.

For a moment she had wondered whether or not the will was genuine, and she had to give up the chance of disputing it, but his words gave her a glimmer of hope. He would surely not make such a claim if he did not feel certain.

'You know the lady, and where she is? Good. Then we can ask her if she signed this, and to give us a sample of her handwriting,' the clerk said. 'That should make it a simple matter, fortunately. How certain are you that it is not her signature?'

'Because I know her writing extremely well. You see, Teresa Kemp is my aunt,' Manuel stated matter-of-factly.

6

'Your aunt?' Janie stared at Manuel, her thoughts in a whirl. 'Then you aren't — you can't be a furniture removal man!'

'Well, no, I'm not.'

'And you let me think — oh, how could you!'

'It seemed simpler.'

'Simpler!' Janie almost exploded.

Her thoughts were chaotic. How had she become entangled in this?

The clerk coughed.

'Miss Tempest, if I could have Mrs Kemp's address, and perhaps her telephone number, I can get on with making enquiries about this will, if she knew anything about it.'

Janie turned back to the important matter. At least it looked as though Brian was mistaken, if not worse, about the will, and her inheritance was safe.

'Oh, I'm sorry. Manuel? I don't know

your aunt's address.'

He took out a pen and wrote the address and telephone number down on a sheet of paper the clerk handed to him. The girl thanked him.

'We'll be in touch, Miss Tempest, but it seems as though you don't have to worry any more.'

Janie muttered something. She was still too stunned by Manuel's revelations that she was incapable of further speech. He took her arm and guided her out, then into a tea-room opposite. After ordering tea and cakes he turned back to Janie, grinning.

'You look as though I'm a ghost, something you can't believe in.'

'Why?' she asked.

'Why did I not tell you at the time?' He laughed. 'Aunt Teresa did her best, if you recall, but I prevented her. If you'd known, would you have let us help you move the furniture?'

Janie shook her head, and laughed.

'No. I'd have been far too embarrassed! Mrs Kemp intimidated me enough, I'd never have dared ask her nephew for a favour. I'm even more in debt to you both now.'

'She's not so bad under that tough surface. We were helping with her last-minute things. The van belongs to Tim. He's an antique dealer, which is why he knew the value of your carpet. He's had it cleaned, by the way, and it's in an auction next week.'

'So if you are not a furniture remover, what are you? An antique dealer as well?'

'No. Tim and I were at college together in the States. My family owns hotels, and I came to Europe to negotiate for some sites here. I rented a flat here because it was near Aunt Teresa. She's my father's only sister.'

Janie could barely take it in. She'd thought Manuel was an ordinary working man, and it seemed he came from a wealthy family who owned hotels all over the world. She forced herself to say something.

'She never mentioned she had

relatives in Mexico. But then, we hardly knew one another.'

'So she told me. She's kind-hearted, but rather a stickler for some of the old-fashioned conventions, like never speaking to anyone unless you've been properly introduced, or wandering round outside in the cold dressed only in a bathrobe!' he added, grinning.

He had a most attractive grin. Janie found it infectious.

'I'm afraid I scandalised her quite a few times in the two years I lived there,' she said ruefully.

'Don't worry. There are more important things to worry about right now, like what's going to happen about Liz's accident. She hasn't heard from the police?'

'Not yet, but there's still time.'

'I think perhaps, if you'll let me, I should go and talk to someone at the Bristol police station. I haven't much time left in England. I have to be in Spain by the end of the month, looking at possible locations there. So let's hope we've sorted out Liz and her problems by then.'

Janie suddenly felt bereft. She was still bemused by the fact that she'd been so horribly mistaken, embarrassed at how she'd made assumptions, grateful that he hadn't disillusioned and disconcerted her at the time, and that he and Tim had helped her with the move. He'd also been a tower of strength coping with Liz's problems, and probably saved time exposing Brian's attempt with the false will for what it was. Her most intense emotion, though, was a sharp stab of disappointment that Manuel would so soon be gone.

She told herself not to be stupid. What did he see in her? They'd met by accident, he'd just been kind, and was probably aching to get away from what must, to him, seem like trivial disputes. Yet here he was proposing to involve himself further.

'Would they talk to you?' she asked doubtfully.

'I think so. I'll go tomorrow. Meanwhile, make sure Liz is more careful. We don't know if Terry is still looking for her. She opened the door to me this afternoon without the chain on, or asking me who I was.'

'She's an idiot! Manuel, why are you being so kind, helping us?'

'I have my own quarrel with Terry, remember, since he saw fit to vandalise my car. I want to see him punished, and make sure he won't try to take it out on you or Liz.'

He refused her invitation to stay for supper, which was perhaps as well, Janie reflected later, when she sat down to scarcely warm baked beans on toast which had been burned and then had the black scraped off.

Afterwards, she tackled Liz about security again.

'You opened the door straight away to Manuel,' she reminded her.

'Yes, but I was expecting him, and I was peeping out of the window. Don't get excited. I was being careful not to be seen. I saw him coming along the road, so I knew who it was. I wouldn't be so daft as to open it if I didn't know who was there. I wouldn't even go to it,' she added virtuously. 'And I can hear who it is on the phone if I leave the answerphone on, and only pick it up if it's Rosa or someone I can trust.'

'Can you trust any of your other friends? Do they know Terry? More importantly, does he know them? Could he be trying to find out where you are through any of them?'

'I don't think he knows anyone apart from Rosa. I only met him a few weeks ago.'

'Who else was at this party? Any of your friends?'

'Not really. A girl who was in the office where I worked before Christmas invited me, but I haven't seen her since, and she didn't know any of my friends.'

'So what do you know about him, or his friends?'

'I've only met Steve, who shares his flat. Oh, and a couple of the others there one night, but I don't know their names. Actually, I think they might have had the flat upstairs.'

Janie left it at that, for she was really tired and had to be up by five. Liz was quieter tonight and did not disturb her, so she was able to sleep well. At the hospital they were short staffed, and she stayed late, so it was early evening before she reached home.

The flat was in darkness, and Janie opened the door as quietly as she could, her heart thumping painfully. Was Liz asleep? Had she gone out? Or had something dreadful happened?

Nothing seemed to be disturbed, and she soon found Liz in the bedroom, lying on the bed, watching television.

'Sorry I'm so late. I didn't even have a chance to phone. How have things been? Any more news?'

'The police phoned this afternoon,' Liz said quietly. 'I don't know if it's good news or bad. But they were rather miffed at me.'

'Why?'

'The car has disappeared. They wanted to check it for defects, they said, but it isn't at Steve's place now. He told them he'd sold it for scrap.'

Janie groaned.

'That was stupid of him! More than stupid, it was criminal.'

'They'll suspect me of trying to cover something up,' Liz said. 'Janie, what can I do?'

'They'll be more likely to charge both you and Steve for obstruction!'

'But I didn't mean to! I was trying to get the car cleared off a busy road! I'd have been obstructing them if I'd just run away and left it there!'

'OK, calm down. Has Manuel rung?'

'No. I expect he's fed up with both of us.'

That would not surprise Janie, but she wanted to know if he'd talked to the police, and if he'd had any luck.

She insisted on cooking supper, despite her tiredness, and was just about to fall into bed when the phone rang. It was Manuel.

'Hi, there, how are you?'

Janie passed on what Liz had told her.

'Did you discover anything?'

'Nothing more, but they've promised to keep me informed, when I stressed the damage Terry did to my car, and mentioned one or two cousins who happen to work in the Embassy.'

Janie laughed.

'You are full of surprises, and have some very useful relatives!'

'I spoke to Aunt Teresa, and she never signed any will, and said she could testify that your Aunt Jane always spoke about you as her heir, right up to her last few days. She never had any time for Brian, my aunt said.'

'That's a relief. So if Liz's exploits don't cost me too much I might be able to afford a house of sorts after all.'

'You know my opinion about helping your feckless sister. Let her sort out her own problems, or she will never grow up, become responsible.'

'If I don't help her, no-one will!'

Janie snapped, her good humour vanishing. 'I've been fortunate.'

'And you feel guilty about it. You shouldn't. You've also worked hard to train for a good profession. But let's not argue. Do you feel fit enough to have dinner tomorrow night? We could make it early to fit in with your shift, so that you are not too late back to bed.'

'I'd love to,' Janie said.

Apart from wanting to see Manuel again, it would be a relief to spend an evening without having to pander to Liz's anxieties. Perhaps she ought to become hard, as he advised. But she knew she couldn't. She'd been Liz's prop for too many years, ever since her little sister, bewildered and homesick, had joined her at their English boarding school while their parents had to live abroad wherever her father's work took them.

Manuel called for her at six and they walked to the same Italian restaurant as before. The head waiter greeted her as though she was an old friend, and Janie relaxed and enjoyed the evening.

Liz was not mentioned until they were drinking coffee. Instead, he told her about his childhood spent in Mexico, visits to England, college in America, and travels all over the world on business since then. He encouraged her to talk about her parents and her own schooldays.

'They live in Malta, now, I think you said,' he prompted.

'Yes. Though he was well paid, my father made some unfortunate investments and lost all his savings. They have just his pension. They couldn't buy a house here when he retired, and after so many years in hot climates my mother couldn't face the English winters anyway. They had a holiday home in Malta, so they live there. I usually manage to go and see them once a year.'

'And Aunt Jane provided a home for you in England?'

'In the short holidays, when it wasn't sensible to fly out for just a few days.

She was my godmother.'

'Not Liz's?'

'No. My mother's sister was Liz's godmother, and we sometimes stayed with her, but unfortunately she died when Liz was sixteen. That's another reason I've felt sorry for her. She adored Aunt Sarah.'

Too soon it was time for Janie to go home.

The rest of the week passed without any further news, either from the police or Manuel. Janie was too weary to care. The settee was proving unsatisfactory as a permanent bed, and when Liz began to hint that she wanted to go back to Bristol, Janie was tempted to agree. Then she told herself not to be silly. A few more days, and surely they would know what was happening, and whether Terry was intending to take any more revenge.

On Saturday, when Janie was luxuriating in a long lie in bed, the doorbell rang with startling urgency.

Liz appeared in the doorway of the

bedroom, looking nervous.

'Who is it?'

'Go back in there, and I'll go and see,' Janie ordered, struggling into her bathrobe.

It was a police constable, and after inspecting his identification, she let him in.

'Do you want to speak with my sister?' she asked.

'Please.'

Liz emerged and sat down on the edge of the settee, sweeping the duvet and pillows on to the floor.

'Miss Tempest, did you know that the car you were driving when you had the accident was stolen?' he asked.

Janie gasped. Liz looked startled.

'No, of course I didn't! Who stole it?'

'The man you borrowed it from, Terry Hughes. The information you gave us about his friend, Steve, enabled us to find him just as he was about to put the car through a compacter. We assume he was intending to destroy the evidence, anticipating that we would want to examine the car. Apparently the two of them had quite a nice little set-up. Your friend, Terry, stole the cars, Steve made the changes, new plates, respray a different colour, new documents, and selling on to unsuspecting customers.'

Liz was incapable of speech. Janie spoke for them both.

'So how does this leave my sister?'

'You knew nothing about this?'

'I've only known Terry a few weeks! He said he was a mechanic, but he didn't say where he worked.'

The constable, a man in his forties, nodded.

'Can you prove that you'd only known him a short while?'

'Rosa could confirm it?' Janie asked, and Liz nodded.

'My flatmate. She'll be able to tell you when I met him.'

He took down further details, then asked if he might use their phone to call Rosa at the flat. After some questions, he seemed satisfied, and rose to his feet.

'I think that will be all for now, thank you, miss.'

'What's going to happen to me?' Liz asked in a small voice.

'That's not up to me, miss, but I don't think you need to worry too much. It's a nice little nest of villains we're going to be dealing with, thanks to your accident.'

7

Janie was on the late shift, which meant she did not reach home until after midnight most nights. Liz fretted, complaining that she would be quite safe if she went out during the daytime, and she didn't see why she could not go home, since Terry and Steve were by now probably in custody. Manuel neither visited nor phoned.

Janie's emotions were a crazy mixture of relief and anxiety. Liz would probably not be charged, Brian's silly attempt to forge a will benefiting himself had been exposed, and she could begin, with some confidence, to look around for a house to buy.

It was partly to escape Liz's constant complaints that Janie went into Bath earlier than she needed every morning, trawling round estate agents collecting house details, and occasionally viewing a house. She admitted to herself, however, that she needed to keep occupied to push thoughts of Manuel to the back of her mind.

It was over now. He had been kind, but had probably found it an irritating business, keeping guard on two women he hadn't even known before the day he helped her to move. She liked him, more than liked him, but she had no hope of interesting a man who came from a wealthy background, travelled the world on business, and was so indecently handsome every woman who met him probably found herself in the same state of hopeless longing.

There was a tiny shred of hope, at least of seeing him again. He still had the old carpet, and when Tim had sold that, surely he would come to give her the money, even if it turned out to be only a few pounds.

He might simply send a cheque, or Tim himself might bring it round. She'd be out at work. And even if by chance they happened to meet, what difference would it make? She'd do far better to forget she'd ever encountered him, and get on with her life.

She'd concentrate on Liz. After this fright her sister might behave more sensibly, and the first step towards this would be to persuade her to find a regular job. Janie began a daily search through newspapers looking for suitable jobs.

It was on Thursday that she found one, in Bath itself, while she was waiting for an estate agent outside a small house in the north of the city. She liked the house, could afford it, and when she rang to arrange for a job interview for Liz the next morning, the woman indicated that she needed someone who could start right away. Liz could live with her, Janie could keep an eye on her, and, she told herself as she drove home that night, dwindle into a sour old maid.

As she pulled up in front of the flats they were in darkness, which was odd. Liz liked late-night TV, and usually sat up watching until Janie came home. If she didn't, she always left the hall light on for Janie. The people upstairs were away. Janie had heard the man talking to the milkman the previous Saturday, stopping the milk for a fortnight, so lack of lights in their flat wasn't unexpected.

As Janie opened the door she could smell smoke through the open living-room door. It didn't smell like cigarettes. That had been her first angry thought, that Liz had somehow had visitors who had left the living-room, her bedroom, impossible to sleep in.

There was barely time for this thought to formulate before, with a startling whoosh of noise, flames began to devour the living-room curtains, outlining the window in a lurid orange flame.

Now Janie could smell petrol. Dropping her bag on the floor she ran through to the bedroom, flicking down the light switch as she went. Nothing happened, but from the glow behind

125

her she could distinguish Liz lying on the bed, on top of her duvet. She was lying unnaturally stretched out.

'Liz, wake up! Come on, you've got to get out. The place is on fire.'

Liz gave a strangled moan, and as Janie moved towards her she saw that her sister was bound, hands tied behind her back, feet together, and a rough gag preventing her from speaking.

There was no time to try and cut her free. Besides, if she had been bound for a long time she'd be too numb to move on her own. Behind her the fire had been growing, the noise of crackling joining the hiss of the flames. Janie slammed the door shut, threw a pillow to prevent some smoke creeping under it, and began to drag Liz towards the window. Fortunately it was a big one, and within seconds she had it open and was pushing Liz through, feet first.

Behind her the smoke was finding its way through the cracks, and Janie began to cough. She heaved herself out of the window, and dragged Liz across the small garden towards the gate in the wall. There she paused, still coughing, and in the faint glow of the street lamps was able to see to untie the knot which secured the gag. The gate was locked, she hadn't a key, and there was no way she could heave Liz over the wall, which was a couple of metres high.

'Oh, Janie, I thought you wouldn't be back in time!' Liz gasped. 'I was so terrified!'

'Never mind. Let me get your legs free.'

The knots were fiendishly tight, and Janie struggled unavailingly for several minutes. In the flat the flames had reached the bedroom, and a lurid glow lit up the tiny garden. Janie sat back, wiping the tears caused by her coughing out of her eyes.

'I'll try your hands,' she gasped between coughs. 'Then you might be able to grab the top of the wall while I heave you over it.'

Liz nodded. She, too, was beginning

to cough as smoke billowed out of the open window.

'He had a key, he must have done, to get in,' she gasped. 'I didn't hear a thing until he was standing behind me. He wore a hood, but it must have been Terry.'

'Never mind that now. Can you try and twist your arms, the way I'm pulling them? That might loosen the strain on your wrists.'

Liz did so, and to her immense relief Janie was able to wiggle the knot and pull one end of the twine that had been used free of it. Within another minute she had the knot undone.

'Listen, that's the fire engine,' Liz said, and Janie lifted her head.

The familiar sirens were getting nearer.

'Then perhaps I won't have to tip you over head first,' she said, silently uttering a prayer of thankfulness. 'When they get here they're bound to try the back, so we'll yell.'

Before there was time for more,

however, there was a crash against the locked gate, then a pounding on it as though someone was attacking it with a battering ram. She dragged Liz back in case the gate gave way and fell on them. Another series of bangs followed, and suddenly the lock broke and the gate swung inwards, hanging crazily on one hinge. Manuel, holding a car jack in one hand and a huge spanner in the other, ran through the gap and almost fell over Liz's feet. His eyes were glittering in the weird glow from the flames in the flat. He stopped abruptly.

'Anyone else in there?' he demanded.

'No,' Janie gasped. 'Can you help Liz? Her feet are tied together.'

He nodded, and handed Janie the spanner and jack. Stooping, he picked up Liz, slinging her over his shoulder, then grabbed Janie's hand and led them through the gateway. Outside they met a couple of firemen dragging a hose.

'Everyone's out,' Manuel said briefly. 'What about the flat upstairs, Janie? The flames have reached there.'

Janie glanced back to see that the upstairs windows were glowing.

'They're away, I'm sure,' she said.

'We'll look to make certain, anyway, miss,' a fireman said.

Manuel nodded and went on.

'Best get out of their way,' he said, still carrying Liz.

Able to breathe more easily, Janie's coughing had stopped and she wiped her eyes again. Manuel's car, his own, she noted, repaired and looking pristine, the driver's door wide open, was slewed across the entrance to the driveway leading to the back of the flats, where some of the residents parked their cars.

'How did you get here?' she gasped as he set Liz down so that she could lean against the bonnet of the car.

'Just driving past. Hang on, Liz, I have a knife somewhere.'

He pulled a small penknife from his pocket, and snapped it open. It was small but sharp, and soon the twine binding Liz's legs together was severed.

'Ouch,' she whispered as the circulation was restored. Janie was already kneeling beside her, massaging her feet.

'It'll be OK in a minute. Don't cry, you're safe now.'

'I'll go and talk to the firemen,' Manuel said briefly, and went towards the front of the flats, where there were sounds of much activity, a police car having arrived to join the fire crew.

'I'll never feel safe again!' Liz wept. 'Janie, he was so nice, I really fell for him, but I'll never dare go back home! He'll follow me everywhere.'

'No, he won't,' Janie soothed her. 'He'll be in prison for even longer after this. We'll have to talk to the police.'

'But where are we going to stay?' Liz wailed. 'Your flat's ruined! And it's all my fault.'

'We can find a hotel, and I'll go and shop for clothes in the morning. I'm almost as badly off as you. All I have is my uniform.'

She thought suddenly about the bag she'd dropped in the hall, with all her

131

credit cards. Unless the firemen had been able to rescue that they'd have problems.

'The firemen have it under control,' Manuel said, suddenly reappearing. 'They'll make it secure, but someone will stay all night to make certain it doesn't flare up again. How are the legs now?'

Liz flexed her ankles.

'OK, thanks. The feeling's come back, and the pins and needles have gone.'

'Good, get in the car, both of you.'

'Can you take us to a hotel?' Janie asked. 'It's too late to do anything else now, and we have nowhere to go.'

'You'll stay at my place.'

'You've a spare room?' Janie asked cautiously.

He turned towards her and she could see the crinkling round his eyes which always indicated amusement. He'd obviously read her thoughts.

'What else?'

'I mean we wouldn't be making you

sleep on a settee,' she said hurriedly.

His flat, the ground floor of a big, Victorian villa, was spacious and furnished with far better quality than the usual rented accommodation. The rooms were large, and still had the original mouldings and cornices. From the hall Janie could see through open doors. There was a living-room, so grand it might be called a drawing-room and two bedrooms. Manuel led the way to the kitchen, well fitted and modern. He filled the kettle.

'I'll get you a dressing-gown, Liz. Then I think we could all do with something to drink. I expect your throats are raw.'

They sat round the pine table drinking hot chocolate, laced with brandy, and Liz told them what had happened.

'I was sitting watching telly, having a drink of cocoa, ready to go to bed, when someone came up behind me and held a knife to my neck. I hadn't heard a thing. He must have had a key.'

'The door was properly locked when I came home,' Janie confirmed. 'No-one had broken in.'

'Skeleton keys, no doubt,' Manuel said, looking grim.

'He gagged me first, then dragged me to the bedroom and tied me up. He wore a hood over his head, with slits for his eyes. It was terrifying. It must have been Terry. I could smell the aftershave he uses, but he never spoke. Then I heard him moving round in the living-room and kitchen, and the front door slammed. A few minutes later I could smell the smoke. I think I passed out from fright, and the next thing I knew was Janie telling me to wake up. Janie, what will he do next?'

'We'll tell the police and hope they can catch him. I'll phone now,' Manuel said. 'He may not have had time to get home. More chocolate?'

'No thanks,' Liz said, suppressing a yawn.

Janie shook her head, too. She hoped Liz was exhausted enough to sleep, but she didn't know if her own jangled nerves would allow her to sink into oblivion.

It was not just the stress of the fire, the fear she had endured as she struggled to get Liz away from the flames. Manuel's sudden reappearance, the surge of delight she had experienced when she heard his voice, had shaken her more than she had expected.

He left the room to phone. A few minutes later he came back to say the police would come and take statements the following morning.

'And then I'll take you to my aunt's. They won't be able to find you there.'

'Mrs Kemp?' Janie asked, startled. 'Won't she object to having us dumped on her?'

'Of course not, and she's close to Warminster, farther away from Bristol, so you'll feel safer there.'

'But surely the police will have arrested Terry before long,' Liz said. 'I'd be safe back in Bristol.'

'And it would be much farther for me to drive into work,' Janie said.

Manuel turned to Liz.

'We don't know if he had anyone else with him. Where was Steve? And is there anyone else involved in this stolen car racket? You'd be safer out of the way until the police have investigated thoroughly, and we are sure there's no-one else out there who bears a grudge.'

'OK. I suppose so.'

'And you'd be better off not going to work for the same reason,' Manuel went on, turning to Janie. 'He may have hoped you'd both be there tonight, and could come after you, too.'

'I can't just not go to work! You know how short of nurses we are, especially at this time of year when people are off sick, and we have more cases coming in with bronchitis and pneumonia! I'll have to stay at a hotel in Bath.'

He argued, pointing out that she would be vulnerable going to and from work if Terry were still at large and knew where she was, but Janie refused to give way.

'Take Liz, and I'm very grateful to you and your aunt, but I won't go.'

'You can stay here then, where I can at least look after you when you're not at work.'

Janie looked at him, too astonished to speak. He grinned.

'Don't worry,' he said softly. 'Now, hadn't you both better get to bed? There are some spare pyjamas in the bedroom, and it has its own bathroom. Sleep well.'

Liz fell asleep the moment she crept into bed, her smoke-grimed T-shirt replaced by a pair of Manuel's pyjamas, deep red silk, and far too large for her. Janie, clad in a similar pair of emerald green pyjamas, lay awake for hours. Had she made the right decision? She was certain that she could not abandon her job but could she cope with living here in Manuel's flat?

It would revive all her anxieties. He had come to rescue them from a sense of duty, and offered them refuge from no other motive than kindness. Ought she to accept, impose even more on him?

She was almost asleep when a new thought brought her wide awake again. How was she to get to work? Her keys were in the abandoned bag, so she couldn't drive unless the bag had been recovered, and from the ferocity of the flames she doubted it would have survived. As far as she could recall she had dropped it near or even inside the living-room, where the fire would have been most fierce.

The fabric would have burned, so would the plastic of her credit cards, and probably the keys would be a melted mass of metal. She couldn't expect Manuel to drive her, and there might not be time to arrange a car hire, even if they would let her have one without any proof of identity or means to pay for it.

Eventually she fell asleep, to be woken the following morning by Liz, her pyjama legs and sleeves rolled up, bringing her a tray with fruit juice, coffee and toast.

'Do you want bacon and egg?' Manuel asked from behind her.

Janie shook her head.

'No, thanks, I'm not exactly hungry. What time is it?'

'Only nine. You have plenty of time to get to work, if you insist on going. I'm thankful I don't have to, even if the alternative is Mrs Kemp. Do you remember the fuss she made last year when we had that barbecue?'

Janie grinned.

'I'm sure you'll find her friendly enough. Manuel says the crustiness is only on the surface!'

Then Janie recalled the job interview she had arranged for Liz that morning, and groaned. She didn't even have the woman's number, and the advertisement from the paper with the phone number was in her handbag, and she couldn't remember the name of the company. In any case, how could Liz attend an interview dressed in borrowed pyjamas?

'I'd better get up,' she decided. 'If Manuel can lend me the bus fare, I may be able to get to Bath in time for work.'

'No need,' Liz said, and went to draw the curtains. 'Come and look.'

On the driveway at the side of the house Janie saw a small red car. She looked at Liz, eyebrows raised.

'How come?'

'Manuel hired it for you. He said your bag was ruined, and everything in it. He'll try and get some more keys for your car today, and he's already asked someone to bring clothes over for us to choose something to wear.'

Janie was beginning to think of all her possessions, lost to the flames or the smoke, and began to mourn her favourite books and clothes. The furniture hadn't been very special, and thank goodness Aunt Jane's antiques were safely in storage. With everything else that had happened, the extra task of replacing things seemed too much.

Resolutely she thrust the problems away from her, and as she luxuriated in a warm, scented bath, thought instead of the problems of coping while she was forced to accept Manuel's offer of somewhere to live.

It would not be easy, given how attracted to him she was, and how unattainable someone like him was for her. He'd ignored them for almost a week, and must be cursing inwardly at being drawn back into their lives with yet more trouble.

She pulled on her uniform, wrinkling up her nose at the lingering smell of smoke. Then she went through to the kitchen, to find Liz eating toast and Manuel leaning back in his chair, holding a mug of coffee in his hands.

He sprang up when she appeared.

'I hope you slept well.'

'Thank you, yes. And Liz showed me the hire car. How did you manage it so quickly?'

'No problem. It was the firm I used

to hire mine from. Come and sit down. More coffee?'

'Thanks, I'd love some. I seem to have a raging thirst.'

'The smoke, no doubt,' he said and held out an envelope. 'Here, take this until you can get your credit cards replaced. Liz says she knows your size, and what you like, so she will choose some clothes for you when the shop sends someone round. Then when she's respectable enough to meet with Aunt Teresa's approval, I'll take her over.'

Janie looked into the envelope and saw at least one hundred pounds. She stared up at him, startled.

'This is far too much. I don't need more than a few pounds.'

'Buy a few pairs of shoes. That's one thing Liz can't try on for you.'

'You are being incredibly kind,' Janie said. 'I couldn't be more grateful. You always seem to be coming to my rescue.'

'The distress does seem to have attacked the damsel rather more than usual,' he replied. 'Here's a spare key in case you get back before I do. What time do you expect to get home?'

'It's late shift, but I often have to stay over if we're short staffed. It's often midnight before I get back. Don't wait up for me.'

'That's late. Would you rather I drove you and fetched you home?'

'No, you've done enough. I'll be fine, don't worry. But I would like to know if Terry's been arrested.'

'I'll ask the police, and I imagine they'll want to interview you and Liz today.'

He was back in her life for the moment, but once this was over he'd soon be going to Spain, and she'd probably never see him again. The more distance she kept between them the easier it would be to forget him when he finally left her.

8

Janie made it just in time to work. She had given into Manuel's insistence that she take the cash and buy some shoes. She could not wear her staid hospital shoes everywhere, but she limited herself to one pair of black low courts which would serve in almost any situation she might find herself in for the next week or so, until her credit cards had been renewed, and insurance sorted out.

A young policeman came to take her statement later that afternoon, but as he was from the local station he had no news to give her about Terry and his likely arrest. They had some emergency admissions towards the end of her shift, so she was late getting away, and it was well after midnight before she reached Manuel's house.

The lights inside were blazing, the

curtains of the living-room open, and Janie saw Manuel standing looking out. Before she switched off her engine, he was opening her car door.

'You're much later than I expected,' he said, and she thought he sounded angry.

'I'm sorry, but we had an emergency. You shouldn't have stayed up!'

'You need a meal. Come on.'

Janie needed her bed, but it seemed churlish to say so when he led her into the kitchen and the delicious smells of hot, spicy food assaulted her senses. She realised she was ravenous. They'd been so busy she hadn't time for more than a quick snack all day.

'Sit down,' he said, pushing her gently into a chair and pouring a glass of red wine.

She watched, revived a little by the wine, as he took a casserole from the oven and ladled beef and carrots and dumplings on to two plates. He put one in front of her and sat down opposite.

It tasted like no beef stew she'd ever

had. He'd used cumin and coriander, he said, and laughed when she told him how unexpected she found the fact that he could cook more than steak.

'I don't like staying in hotels when I'm working abroad, and I don't want to eat out every night, nor can I exist on baked beans and Chinese takeaways. So I had to learn to cook.'

'How is Liz?'

He chuckled.

'She had a wonderful time choosing new clothes, but you can see what she chose for you in the morning. When I left her, she and Aunt Teresa were getting on like the proverbial house on fire, though perhaps that isn't the best simile to use!'

'Liz was terrified of your aunt before. What changed?'

'Liz saw a book about the Knights of Malta on the coffee table. Aunt Teresa's going there later in the year. Liz began to say that the Knights had not been the saints people usually think, Aunt Teresa disagreed — she's a romantic at heart — and I left them hotly debating the history and morality of the Crusades.'

Janie laughed.

'Liz has spent far more time in Malta than I have, and my father's a bit of a fanatic about the island's history.'

Suddenly she yawned.

'Sorry. That was delicious, but I must get to bed. Thank goodness tomorrow's Saturday.'

There was a glamorous silk night-dress laid out in the bedroom, and Janie eyed it with some suspicion. If this had been Liz's choice, she wondered what her sister had selected for daytime wear, but she was too tired to care.

A few moments after she woke to weak February sunshine pouring in through the windows, she went through to the kitchen.

'Breakfast,' Manuel said briskly. 'It's midday, you have to inspect your new clothes and shop for more. I'm taking you into Bristol.'

'I'm sure I don't need more and I don't think going to Bristol's a good idea, not while Terry is still at large. I suppose you've heard nothing.'

'The police rang to say Steve had been apprehended, but Terry has vanished. You needn't be afraid, though. I'll be with you.'

'Let me see what Liz chose for me first, after I've had that coffee.'

For the rest of that day, Janie's thoughts were in turmoil. Manuel was friendly but businesslike.

She approved of the clothes Liz had chosen for her, but they were all very smart suits and dresses. There was nothing Janie felt suitable for everyday wear, no jeans or T-shirts. Reluctantly she agreed to go to Bristol and even more reluctantly bought twice as much as she had intended.

'It will save time. You need them,' Manuel insisted, retrieving the items she had handed back to the salesgirl. 'You lost everything.'

The car was laden with parcels and

when she had unpacked everything, Janie found that the bag from the chemist's with her shampoo and face cream, lip gloss and talc, also contained a huge box of expensive perfumes, in small fancy sample bottles. She went to find Manuel in the living-room.

'I didn't buy this,' she said, holding the box out to him.

'No, it's a present from me. I don't know what you like, so I bought a selection.'

'You're being so generous! I feel I'm taking advantage.'

'Nonsense. Now put on that blue dress Liz chose for you, like the one you wore the day we met, and we'll go out for dinner. And we are invited to Aunt Teresa's for Sunday lunch.'

The rest of the weekend passed in a blur. Liz pounced on her the moment they reached Mrs Kemp's house on the Sunday, saying excitedly that a friend of Mrs Kemp's wanted a secretary to help her with a book of memoirs she was writing, both to do research and help her type up her copious notes and diaries.

'Lady Gordon is so sweet. She was staying here, but she had to go home early this morning. I'll live with her, near Salisbury, for at least six months.'

'Leaving Bristol and all your friends there?' Janie asked rather sceptically.

'I can visit them at weekends if I want, but I see now that apart from Rosa and her crowd, they weren't much good. Many of them were like Terry,' she admitted, rather shamefacedly. 'Has he been caught?'

'Not yet, but Steve has, and no doubt they'll soon flush him out from wherever he's hiding.'

Janie was still on the late shift, but she saw less of Manuel. He had managed to get replacement keys for her own car, so the hired car was sent back. He had usually gone out by the time she got up in the morning, but he always had a hot meal waiting when she got back in the evenings. It was on

Friday that life was once more thrown into turmoil.

She was returning form the hospital canteen when she heard an altercation in the ward office. A man was shouting, and Janie ran towards the noise. They sometimes had abusive patients or distraught relatives to deal with, and she knew that the other nurse, Trisha, was alone.

A man in his twenties, tall and with regular features, was leaning over the desk, shouting at Trisha who was pinned into her chair and couldn't move away from him.

'I know she works here, and she's let me and my mates in for a load of trouble, so don't give me that innocent look. Tell her I'll get her, one day, and her sister, when I find her. The boyfriend can't be with her all the time!'

As Janie paused in the doorway, certain this was Terry Hughes, a couple of security men ran past her and grabbed him by the arms.

151

'Come along now, we can't be upsetting patients, can we?' one said as they led a resisting Terry away.

Janie slipped into a convenient storeroom. It would do no good for Terry to see her, and her help wasn't needed. She was thinking furiously. It must be Terry and somehow he'd tracked her down.

Trisha had collapsed into tears of fright, and it took Janie a while to calm her. She was fretting at the delay, but rang the security office as soon as Trisha blew her nose and said she could cope. She meant to ask them to hang on to Terry and call the police, who wanted him, only to be told that he had been ejected from the hospital seconds before, and they had seen him drive off in a big estate car.

She must warn Manuel at once. She rang him and luckily he was at home. Rapidly explaining the situation she begged him to take care.

'Don't worry,' he said calmly.

'But he might damage your car again!'

'Then I'll garage it and hire one. I'll get the smaller one back for you as well, just in case he knows your car. The police have one bit of news you'd be interested in, though. Brian Cook has been arrested.'

'Brian? Why? Because of the forged will?'

'No. One part of the operation was the theft of cars to order, the expensive sports cars and so on, and Brian was involved in transporting them abroad once Steve had changed the colour and filed off the obvious registration marks.'

'Brian, a crook?'

'So it seems.'

'So him being at the same party where Liz met Terry wasn't pure coincidence. What about Christine? She works in a travel agency.'

'Does she? I think the police might be interested in that. She wasn't averse to a spot of deception over that fake will. Now, I'm coming to fetch you home tonight. Wait somewhere safe inside the hospital.'

Janie bristled at his imperious tone, but at the same time was feeling more confident. She had been worrying about being followed home, if Terry waited around until she had finished her shift. He seemed obsessed enough to do it. She didn't know how much he knew about her, whether he knew her in person, but the news that Brian was involved with him made it more likely that he'd have obtained information about her from Brian, who had his own grudge against her.

For once her shift finished on time, and she sat in the staff canteen until one of the porters brought Manuel in.

Manuel ushered Janie out to where a large, oldish-looking Rover was parked in the bays reserved for consultants.

They were halfway home, Janie dozing, when she was shaken awake as Manuel swung the car round a sharp corner, accelerating away as fast as he could.

'What is it?' she gasped.

'I suspect we're being followed. I just

want to check. Yes, he passed the road, then reversed and turned in. Right, Mr Hughes, we'll lead you a dance.'

Janie watched through the rear window as Manuel did his best to shake off the pursuing car, but the Rover was neither as fast nor as manoeuvrable as his own car, and the estate car behind managed to keep up with him, but never getting close enough to be dangerous.

They twisted through the lanes, sped through villages, ignoring all speed limits, and Janie, clinging to her seat, wished heartily for a police patrol car to appear. None did, of course. As Manuel turned into a steep lane leading up into the hills, he gave a grunt of satisfaction.

'Good, I recognise this place,' he said, and changed down to a low gear.

The lane was steep and twisting, winding through a dense wood that shut out all light from the distant glow of Bristol. Then they came to a dip, and Manuel switched off his lights and turned into a narrow lane at the bottom, swinging off it immediately into a sandy track. He switched off the engine, rolled his window down a crack, and they waited.

The other car's engine was straining, and then eased as it came to the dip. They saw the gleam of the headlights swinging past, and disappearing over the far hump out of the dip. They reappeared a second later, turning and twisting as the car negotiated bends, and as it was now downhill, the car increased speed.

Then they heard the squeal of brakes, and the headlights swung in an arc high above the wood before the sound of the car crashing into trees reached them. The lights spun, then came to rest, pointing straight up into the sky.

'He's crashed over the edge,' Manuel said. 'Stay here. I'll go and see.'

'He might be hurt. I'm coming.'

He reached into the glove compartment for a torch, but didn't switch it on. Janie could just distinguish the track between the trees, and Manuel grasped her hand and led her back towards the road. The rain was heavy, but they had a little shelter from the branches above. On level ground, they broke into a run and reached the spot where the estate had left the road, to be almost blinded with the light from the headlamps.

Manuel shone the torch round, but all they could see were trees and mangled bushes. The estate car seemed to have come to rest at a crazy angle against the trunk of a big tree, after sliding and somersaulting twenty metres or so down the slope.

'Let's get out of the glare of the lights, then we can see if he's still inside.'

Cautiously they scrambled down the steep slope, slippery from the rain, clutching at bushes to control the descent. Manuel shone his torch towards the car, and they could see someone hanging out of the driver's door, which had partially ripped away, caught up in the seat-belt.

'Stay here, direct the torch for me, and ring the emergency services. The car might blow up any minute,' Manuel ordered, and before Janie could protest he'd thrust the torch into her hands and was sliding down towards the car.

Struggling to keep the torch beam steady, Janie dragged her mobile phone out of her pocket and, one-handed, punched in the numbers. She had only the vaguest idea where they were, but when she described the place, and mentioned the name of a village they'd passed through, the policeman said he thought he knew where it was.

Half her attention had been on Manuel, and she'd seen him reach the car and lean in to release the seat-belt. Then he grasped the man by the shoulders and began to ease him out.

Janie had feared he might be dead, but as Manuel moved him, he let out an agonised scream. She slithered down the slope, knowing Manuel would need help.

'His foot's caught under one of the

pedals, and I suspect his legs are broken,' Manuel said calmly. 'Can you support him while I get in the other side and try to get him free?'

Janie nodded, and took Manuel's place. Terry's screams had diminished and he was alternately groaning and sobbing. She had time to notice that petrol was seeping from the ruptured tank, and thankful it was running away from them. It was still a danger, but possibly a lesser one than if it had been coming towards them.

At last Manuel managed to wrench the pedal free and Janie pulled Terry farther out of the car. Manuel clambered back to take over from her, and between them they eased him out.

'We've got to get him farther away in case it blows up,' Manuel panted. 'There's no time to make a stretcher. We'll just have to drag him.'

'Let me see if I can do anything. It looks as though both legs are broken and you're bleeding badly,' Janie said, stooping down to look. 'Manuel, can you hold the torch for me, please?'

She leaned over Terry to pass the torch to Manuel.

'You think you've won!' Terry snarled, and before Janie could dodge, he'd lashed out at her with a clenched fist.

The blow caught her on the side of the head, she lost her balance, and felt herself tumbling headlong down the slope. She grabbed frantically at bushes, but none of them was sturdy enough to break her fall, and for a desperate moment she wondered just how far down she had to go.

She heard a shout, and crashing noises which didn't seem to be her own, then there was an explosion and above her to the left, the car burst into flames. She felt the speed of her descent lessening, and came to an abrupt halt against a sturdy sapling, knocking all the breath out of her body.

Struggling to breathe, she felt arms round her and Manuel's voice close to her ear.

'Janie, querida, are you all right? I'll break every other bone in his body if he's hurt you!'

She gasped. 'I think I'm OK, just winded.'

He helped her sit up, and sat beside her, his arm both supporting and comforting her.

'At least the fire service will be able to find us,' Janie said, looking at the blazing car. 'Are we far enough away to be safe?'

'Yes, it's still pouring with rain and everywhere is so wet there's no chance of the trees and bushes catching fire. And I think I heard a siren a moment ago. Listen. Yes, there it is again.'

'We really should climb back up,' Janie said, but reluctantly.

She had just realised that Manuel had called her darling, in Spanish. Had he meant it, or had he used the word as one would to a child in a moment of stress? She wanted to think about this, but the sirens were getting louder, and they didn't want to cause more work for

161

the firemen by letting them search for the other victims.

Half-an-hour of frenzied activity followed. When they had pulled themselves up to the spot where they'd left Terry, they found an ambulance crew lifting him on to a stretcher.

Janie insisted she was quite all right, and did not need to go to the hospital. All she wanted were a hot bath and clean dry clothes. Manuel told a rather sceptical policeman that Terry was wanted by his colleagues in Bristol.

'We'll get home,' Manuel said, and, keeping his arm round Janie, began to guide her along the lane to where they'd left his car.

They had dropped the torch when Terry attacked Janie, and though Manuel had retrieved it later, it was broken. Fortunately the moon had emerged from behind the clouds, they could make out the wet surface of the road, and soon got to their car.

Manuel produced a rug from the

boot and tucked it round Janie, then made her drink from a small brandy flask he had in the glove compartment. He started the car, turned the heater on full, and edged his way cautiously back on to the track and then the road. Within twenty minutes they were back at his flat.

'Have a hot bath, and after I've changed I'll make us a drink,' Manuel said, and Janie was left alone.

Her uniform was filthy, covered in mud and dead leaves, with streaks of blood which must have come from Terry, and she stripped it off quickly and threw everything into a plastic sack. She'd wash it the next day. She was unscathed apart from a few scratches and bruises, but she ached, and the soft-scented water lulled her almost to sleep. She came to when Manuel knocked on the door to ask if she was all right.

'Yes, thank you. I'll be out in a few minutes,' she called, heaving herself out of the bath and wrapping a thick towel about her body.

She dried herself, raked her fingers through her wet hair, and put on the big towelling robe, then went slowly towards the kitchen. She was feeling unaccountably shy. Had Manuel meant that endearment? She recalled the touch of his arms about her, the comfort and warmth of him, the subtle scent of his aftershave, and felt a mixture of trepidation and hope.

He was in the kitchen, dressed in jeans and a thin white sweatshirt which clung to his muscular body. His hair was tousled, and he looked more devastating than ever, especially when he smiled at her.

'Come and sit down, querida.'

She glanced up at him, a question in her eyes, and he set a mug of coffee down before her. He grinned, rather ruefully.

'Hadn't you guessed?'

'Guessed?'

'That I'm crazy about you. It was no part of my plan to fall in love. I travel too much to have a stable home life. No woman would put up with it. I tried to break away from you, to tell myself it was just a temporary attraction, but it's no good. I love you and nothing else matters. How about you? Could you love me, do you think?'

He took her hands in his, and Janie found herself being slowly pulled to her feet.

'Yes,' she said softly, 'I feel the same, but I didn't dare hope you'd ever think of me. You must know loads of glamorous women.'

'But none who come rushing out to me in bath robes,' he said, and chuckled, pulling her into his arms and bending his lips towards hers. 'By the way, Tim sold your carpet, and the cheque came for you this morning. It raised even more than he'd predicted. Shall I fetch it?'

'No!' Janie exclaimed, and grabbed his hair in both hands, pulling his face closer. 'Kiss me.'

He did as she asked, very thoroughly,

and she was breathless by the time he released her.

'Will you take me on? I shall hand over my job to my younger brother, José, and he can do the travelling. I will run the office here in England, and if you want to carry on nursing I can set it up in Bath. I'll go away just a couple of times a year to make inspections, and take you with me, for I can't be parted from you now.'

Janie gave him her answer by reaching up and kissing him again.

'I don't want to be parted from you, ever,' she murmured.

'An Easter wedding? That just about gives us time to tell our friends and get our families over here. Aunt Teresa will have the reception. She told me to tell you when we saw her last Sunday.'

'Your aunt? But she doesn't like me! And how did she know?'

He laughed.

'She's like a marshmallow inside, and I'm her favourite nephew. She has said for years now that it was time I married. When we delivered her furniture she took me to one side and recommended that I grabbed you before anyone else did.'

Janie laughed.

'I'd never have believed it.'

'True. But I don't like my life being run for me, so I resisted, against my instincts. We'll go out and visit her tomorrow. She can start organising the marquee and the caterers, unless your mother would prefer to do it.'

'She would, I'm sure, but it would be a problem from Malta.'

'Then your parents can come and stay with her and they can manage it between them. All I care about is spending as much time with you as I can. Janie, promise me you'll never tangle with crooks like Terry Hughes again.'

'I promise!'

'I'll be making sure of it,' he teased.

We do hope that you have enjoyed reading this large print book.

Did you know that all of our titles are available for purchase?

We publish a wide range of high quality large print books including:
Romances, Mysteries, Classics
General Fiction
Non Fiction and Westerns

Special interest titles available in large print are:
The Little Oxford Dictionary
Music Book, Song Book
Hymn Book, Service Book

Also available from us courtesy of Oxford University Press:
Young Readers' Dictionary
(large print edition)
Young Readers' Thesaurus
(large print edition)

For further information or a free brochure, please contact us at:
Ulverscroft Large Print Books Ltd.,
The Green, Bradgate Road, Anstey,
Leicester, LE7 7FU, England.
Tel: (00 44) **0116 236 4325**
Fax: (00 44) **0116 234 0205**

SUMMER IN HANOVER SQUARE

Charlotte Grey

The impoverished Margaret Lambart is suddenly flung into all the glitter of the Season in Regency London. Suspected by her godmother's nephew, the influential Marquis St. George, of being merely a common adventuress, she has, nevertheless, a brilliant success, and attracts the attentions of the young Duke of Oxford. However, when the Marquis discovers that Margaret is far from wanting a husband he finds he has to revise his estimate of her true worth.